The Black River

The Black River

Jovon Scott with Larry L. Franklin

To order additional copies of this book, contact:
Xlibris
844-714-8691
www.Xlibris.com
Orders@Xlibris.com
815373V

CONTENTS

ACKNOWLEDGMENT

I would like to give a special thanks to my editor, Larry L. Franklin, for encouraging me to grow as a writer, and for the long hours put in on editing this project. Thank you!

Chonice Brown and Maurice Scott, I appreciate y'all for holding things down and keeping my relevance beyond these walls. I love you both!

Celeste and Tanisha, thank you for the years of support and always having my back.

Ashley Gardner, you're a very special woman and i love you more than life. A.N.Y & ALWAYS!

Torri Brown, I'm proud of the woman you've become, and I look forward to seeing you accomplish more in the near future.

Fendi Frost, Lil Mil and Brandon Lewis, I appreciate y'all being solid and giving me hope for the days to come. My dude Fendi, you're about as solid as they come.

Tianna Cooks, thank you for believing in me, I wish you nothing but happiness.

Janece Rosenthal, I love u with all that's humanly possible. Keep you sense of humor and your relentless personality. When I find my freedom, I'll find you and be sure to express my gratitude.

To my future wife and best friend, Renim Arreis. You blew through my life like a relentless storm and made a strong impression that pulled me all the way in. Loving you would be easy, and I look forward to spending my life with you. I appreciate you trusting me and giving me the opportunity from such a hopeless place.

Georgette Hill, I love you forever!

R.I.P to the great Kobe Bryant. You inspired me from a distance and taught me what it meant to have a mamba mentality off the court. 8 and 24 forever!!

Blueprint writer's group, grit, grind, and hustle.

NOTE FROM THE AUTHOR

This is a work of fiction, a psychological thriller to be exact. The fact that it could have happened is not that far-fetched. Any time we delve into the mysteries of the human mind, we marvel at our saneness. After all, the human brain has over 100 billion nerve cells called neurons that communicate with other neurons through a substance called neurotransmitters. This enables us to do all of the things that we consider humanly possible — drink a cup of coffee, climb a mountain, or if we're one of the lucky ones, calculate the size of the universe. It is here where sanity and insanity are controlled by DNA, life experiences, medication, street drugs, sex, and fate.

The human brain serves as the hotbed for Dr. Tianna Smith's behavior; a psychologist and main character of this story who suffers from a serious mental illness. Each character is pictured as a sane individual with the typical social interactions humans face. As the story develops, the secrets will gradually unfold, providing the reader with a clear understanding of *"The Black River."*

PROLOGUE

Victoria watched the rough-water hug the riverbank. The sun retired for the day and the river gave birth to short bursts of waves that threatened the shore. Mother Nature's elements of tranquility and destruction were on full display. Victoria's eyes pierced the water's surface as she studied the river snaking through pastures and open plains. Barricades dared not to confine its flow.

When Victoria was young, large bodies of water threatened her well-being. So much so that she barred herself from diving into the mysteries that lie below the river's surface. Time revealed the reason for her fears. Someone or something lived in the darkened waters that threatened her safety. But don't blame Victoria for having a dysfunctional childhood and an overly creative mind. Her brain was hardwired to think irrationally.

Something was off that day; a gut-wrenching and unnerving kind of off. Victoria blamed herself for what happened when she met Chanel at the river. While all of the signs were there, it was a time of confusion when 2 equals 1.

"Are you scared?" Chanel asked. "You're shaking."

Victoria knew that she was afraid. As the two of them stood on the water's edge watching the currents race by, there was an eerie silence. Victoria didn't know why, but she had told Chanel that she wasn't afraid.

Chanel had an energy that was quite alluring; an adrenaline junkie who danced along the edges of danger. Each adventure was accompanied by a spiritual energy as if she was suddenly reborn. Her breathing became more labored and her heart was on fire. Victoria grabbed Chanel's hands that were cold and unwelcoming as if she had touched a stranger. They faced each other; so close that their heartbeats were in unison. As their lips touched, Victoria remembered the passion that burned deep into her soul; spellbound and persuaded by the words that Chanel never spoke; eyes that shared a telling tale; and private things that remained hidden from the world.

Chanel's demeanor morphed into an emptiness disconnected from reality. Is this the person who Victoria had known to be Chanel, or was she an illusion?

"Do you love me?" Chanel questioned. She gripped Victoria's hand tighter as if she dared her to tell a lie.

"Of course, I love you," Victoria answered. But the grip of Chanel's hand was different, causing Victoria to wonder if Chanel had become a complete stranger. At the moment, Victoria did not fear the river. She was more afraid of the entity she perceived to be Chanel.

"Why would you ask if I loved you?" Victoria asked.

"Because I need to know."

"Yes, I love you. But you know that already. You're acting strange and freaking me out," Victoria admitted.

Chanel's laugh was accompanied by a sinister smile. "If you love me, jump, jump into the river," Chanel commanded. "Love is all about trust, right?"

"I will drown," Victoria replied. "I can't swim, you know that."

"Trust me," Chanel explained. "I would never allow anything bad to happen to you."

Victoria felt overcome by emotions knowing that she needed to escape before it was too late. While she remembered fragments of what happened that day, she preferred to believe that Chanel pushed her into the river. Given Victoria's fear of the river, that made more sense. But reality told a different story. Victoria jumped into the river.

Stupidity is oftentimes driven by ignorance, a compelling force that causes us to defy logic. Perhaps a need to display her courage was why Victoria jumped into the river, or was it love interlinked with confusion?

A blind fondness accompanied by faith creates the foundation for love. But reckless love ignores your core, leaving you to think only of the image you desire; the one that caused Victoria to jump into the river.

Chanel stood on the shore watching Victoria struggle to evade the adversity she had feared since her childhood — drowning in the river. Her attempts to scream were muffled by the sheer volume of water. Most people who fear the possibility of death by drowning, stay away from large bodies of water. But not Victoria, she jumped into the river.

Victoria's mind held no clarity or reasoning for what was happening to her. She felt the burning sensation a body experiences when your lungs take on water. The image of the river changed as she began to accept her fate. The deeper parts of the river were calm and without motion, unlike the chaotic movements of the river's surface. The struggle to survive diminished as her body sank towards the river's floor.

Victoria remembered seeing Chanel through the water's surface; lips parted with a smile on her face. At that moment Victoria's heart stopped beating; not from drowning but from a broken heart. Chanel killed Victoria before the water filled her lungs and severed her oxygen supply.

She then experienced a more peaceful world as her body embraced the river's floor. She looked up through the surface and saw Chanel standing at the water's edge. No longer angered. Victoria was at peace. Now as Victoria accepted her fate, she saw the two of them standing side by side; both one in the same, when 2 equals 1.

CHAPTER ONE

Chanel

ONE YEAR EARLIER:

It was in the early hours of the morning when the city was stirring with party-goers, drug addicts, and the homeless who were looking for a place to sleep. Except for a few travelers on their way home, the streets were filled with police cars and ambulances looking to salvage another night in the city.

An ambulance raced down the streets with lights flashing and sirens blasting, hoping to make it to the Mount Rush Hospital in time. The paramedic in the back of the ambulance told the driver to go faster; the woman might not survive.

"We have a female patient suffering from a drug related overdose, believed to be heroin," the paramedic said as the patient was being moved from the ambulance to the emergency room. A doctor entered the room and flashed a light into the woman's eyes to determine if they were dilated; a common symptom for a drug overdose.

"Get an I.V. going. I need her vitals asap. Start the reversal drug immediately," the doctor ordered as the medical staff went to work, knowing that there was a small window to save her. While the woman's pulse was faint, she was still alive. Her name was Chanel Rosenthal.

"Chanel, how much did you take?" the doctor asked. "I need to know." As the nurse added the solution to her I.V., Chanel responded in gibberish. She then leaned over the bed and vomited onto the floor. This was a typical day for Chanel. She frequently found herself in the Mount Rush Emergency Room where the doctors and nurses knew her well.

Chanel found these roller coaster rides to be exhilarating. She cherished the altered state of mind, shifting from one reality to another. For her, the drug overdose was mind blowing; releasing the beatitudes that opened the path to a spiritual awakening; and being on the edge, the place that society deemed to be life threatening. Chanel wasn't naive, she knew her chosen path was destructive and insanely suggestive. She asked only for the freedom to be herself.

Hours passed before Chanel opened her eyes. She scanned the room as memories of her night flashed through her mind. While only fragments, they began to tell a story: Chanel had gone to one of her favorite clubs, listened to music, had drinks topped off with coke, followed by a heavy dose of heroin. She was no stranger to blackouts or being strapped to hospital beds after drug overdoses. Although she had teased death on multiple occasions, killing herself was not a conscious choice. She just loved being high, drunk, and the short bursts of ecstasy driven by emotional orgasms.

The thought of death had never discouraged Chanel from her chosen lifestyle. While she barely survived many life-threatening experiences, there were no regrets. Circumstances had always returned her to the living. Her mind had been plagued with so much trauma and torment that an adjustment of her brain's wiring was an escape.

Except for the fact that they had been killed, Chanel knew nothing about her parents. The man who raised her was a father figure, providing her with a different perspective on fatherhood. When he died, Chanel was placed into foster care, another life experience gone amiss. This was where Chanel's young mind was introduced to the ugly side of life.

The poverty-stricken slums of Chicago catered to degenerates and the altered minds of most adolescences. The child-care system was the equivalent to a prison for children. Chanel embraced her rebellious ways and became the epitome of a destructive, unpredictable teenage menace; possibly the worst case in the group home. When Chanel turned 18, psychologists and psychiatrists considered her to be socially disconnected from reality.

As time passed, Chanel became engrossed in drugs and sex while chasing that first high; a high that she could never match no matter how hard she tried. Despite the drug abuse, Chanel was a beautiful woman. Her appearance was the ultimate bait in convincing men to play out her lifestyle. While it was a reflection of her behavior, she never thought of it as being repugnant. Sex was only a deflection allowing her to dissociate from her conscious thoughts.

Chanel's five-foot five-inch frame, shoulder-length hair, and thick lips added to her sex appeal. Perhaps her dark-colored eyes accompanied by an alluring gaze were the ultimate mystery that grabbed your attention.

"Chanel Rosenthal, I guess you must like us here at the Mount Rush Hospital?" Nurse Jamie asked as she and the doctor walked into the room.

"I'm thinking that you have a thing for me, Doc. We can't keep meeting like this," Chanel joked with a half-hearted smile.

"Are you trying to kill yourself or are you just in dire need of some attention?" the Doctor asked.

"Now you sound like Doctor Phil. Dying isn't easy for me. I've tried more times than you can imagine," Chanel replied.

The Doctor proceeded to make his case for survival. "Maybe self-sabotaging isn't for you. I can tell you next time you try to kill yourself, you may succeed. Here's something you need to do for yourself, stop using. Look at this x-ray."

The Doctor held the film up to the light. "If you look near the heart, you'll notice a dark area the size of a golf ball. That's called an aneurysm, which is a blood-filled bulge in your blood vessel. If this were to erupt, you'd die from eternal bleeding. It's a miracle that it hasn't already killed you. You don't need surgery. It'll go away on its own if your heart isn't forced to do unnecessary work. When you shoot drugs, it forces your body to regulate the body temperature, heart rate and other things. So, if you want to live, no more drugs. I can give you information on where to find help, but you already know these things."

"I didn't know it was that bad," Chanel answered with a measure of concern.

"Yeah, it's very bad," the Doctor replied. "You're young and beautiful with your entire life ahead of you. Make something of it and do yourself a favor, stay alive." With that said the doctor left Chanel to think about her mortality. She closed her eyes and explored her thoughts. She didn't want to die. While she didn't have a lot to live for, maybe one day that would change. She at least owed herself that. She'd never attempted to quit, but the stories she heard from recovering addicts was something she wasn't ready to experience. It's a shame how people don't get the chance to choose who brings them into this world. Her mother was dead, and her father was a piece of dysfunctional shit. When Chanel felt a tear fall from her eye, it became real. Only Chanel could save herself.

*   *   *

"You're a hard woman to catch up with. I thought you forgot about me and ran away," John said as he opened the door to the hotel room that he and Chanel often used. Her short dress and red heels added to the seductive strut in her effortless strides.

"I find ways to keep myself busy, besides, you're here now," replied John, a highly paid criminal defense attorney and married man. John often times spent evenings with escorts and call girls. That was until he met Chanel who made such an everlasting impression that John only wanted her.

"You know, I don't like it when you're unavailable. My time is limited," John said. He removed his suit jacket and sat on the edge of the bed. Chanel leaned against the dresser and just looked at him. Her behavior illustrated the fact that John needed her touch.

"How bad do you want me?" Chanel asked as she began to unbutton her blouse.

"Bad. I want you now. I thought about you all weekend when I was with my wife," John admitted. While Chanel's breasts were not overly large, they were full, firm, and perky.

"I think you can wait a while longer before I allow you to touch me," Chanel teased.

"Please don't make me wait. I'll do anything," he pleaded. Chanel stripped down to her bra and panties. His mouth watered with anticipation. She looked into his eyes that were filled with lustful-intentions. John's erection was about to burst out of his pants.

Chanel placed one of her legs on top of his thighs and pulled her panties to the side, giving him access. John tasted her and then inserted two fingers inside her slit. She let out a sigh and bit down on her bottom lip. She was never in the business of pleasing herself. This was her job, but for John it was different.

Chanel allowed herself to be drawn into the moment. John removed her panties and pulled her ass-cheeks apart to get deeper into her wet tunnel. Chanel then moved away from him and got on her knees, undid his belt and removed his pants. Once she had his penis in her hand, she looked him in the eyes and swallowed him whole. The sensation of having her grab his penis combined with the warmth of her mouth made his toes curl. Chanel stroked his length all while sucking and keeping a rhymical motion. John was about ready to burst, but he stopped himself and pulled Chanel to her feet. She left the room to retrieve a condom from her handbag. She opened it up and put the condom inside of her mouth and returned to him. Chanel then swallowed the length of his shaft until the condom covered it completely. She undid her bra, allowing her breasts to hang freely. She then climbed into the bed and spread her legs enough for John to experience her world of bliss.

When John got on top and made penetration, her mind shifted into another realm. So many things filled her thoughts. Memories of the conversation with the doctor after her last overdose replaced her sexual desires. Withdrawing from her sexual encounters was not unusual for Chanel, or for anyone with a history of sexual abuse. Her father had fucked that part of Chanel a long time ago.

When John finished, he cleaned himself up and left. For a while she reflected on the things that brought her to this point, the place she defined as her identity. Chanel called her dealer and waited for him to deliver her next fix.

Some thirty-minutes later, Chanel was cooking her heroin on a spoon; anxious to enter her alternative reality if only for a short time; and fully aware that she could cause more damage to her body. But for Chanel, the thought of sobriety was the closest thing to being dead. Chanel spread her toes and found a spot to insert the needle. She often described the abrupt sensation as a rush of waves crashing into the side of a ship, moving her into a state of ecstasy. This was her "happy place," a place void of negative energy.

*   *   *

I danced along the shadows of death,
and smiled at life as if nothing was left.
Just me and all of my misery,
I danced along the shadows of death,
as I trade my shares of sanity to proclaim
what was left of my ties to vanity.
Death called and I answered,
we talked for hours.
Conveying our thoughts and conversing like lost souls.
Death really cared about me.

I danced along the shadows of death
as if nothing was left.
Death cradled me with passion
as the warmth from the ashes burned away the sadness.
That's why I dance in the shadows,
along the side of death,
Because it was all that I had — all that was left.

CHAPTER TWO

Victoria

Winnipeg was home for massive trees and soaring mountains; a place where nature was untamed. Rivers cut through the countryside without regard to what lie ahead. By any definition, Canada was beautiful.

"Mr. Butler, how long have you known me?" Victoria asked her butler, Mr. Holmes. While James Holmes was his given name, he answered to Mr. Butler.

"I've known you since you were a little girl with very big eyes and a long nose I might add."

"Would you consider me to be self-centered and somewhat disconnected?" Victoria questioned.

"I think you're living according to the rules that fit you," Mr. Butler said. "You have a great deal of responsibility for a young lady, and with that comes questions that you already have the answers to."

"Sometimes I think I know my purpose and in an instance, I have no idea. It's like my brain shuts down," Victoria explained.

"You're only twenty. You have more time to figure things out. Live a little and make a few mistakes along the way. Don't be bound by the expectations of your mother," he said.

"I think you chose the wrong profession," Victoria said. "You should have been a philosopher. You're wise and equally kind. Yes, you should have been a philosopher."

"What makes you think that I'm not?" Mr. Butler replied with a wink of his eye as he walked away.

Victoria had grown lonesome since her mother died a few years ago. She had never experienced a connection with children her own age. Victoria's thoughts were interrupted by a telephone call.

"I'm sorry to bother you Ms. Bloom. My name is Samantha Westros and I'm calling about the charity event. Since your mother was a major supporter, we decided to keep her name on the guest of honors list. Your company has donated more than $10 million to our cause. Are you planning on attending the event on her behalf?"

"When is it?" asked Victoria.

"April 3rd in Sault Ste. Marie, the grand ballroom on 5th Avenue."

"I'll have someone contact you and give you an answer. I need to look at my schedule," explained Victoria.

"Oh, one more thing. It's a masquerade party," Samantha added.

"Duly noted." With that in mind, Victoria ended the call. While Victoria was not like her mother, they were best friends. Her mother was more into the glitter of high society while craving the lime-light.

Although her mother's name was Elana Bloom, Victoria called her Lana. It was common practice for Victoria to call those close to her by a nickname. Growing up in a mansion that sat on eighty acres of land, and being the only child, led to boredom. She was born into a wealthy family, providing Victoria with every materialistic thing she desired. Lana hid her daughter from the rest of the world; shielding her from the chaos that society offered. She was home-schooled and in the eyes of her mother, raised in the best way possible. But Victoria just wanted a normal childhood.

Now, as an adult, Victoria was adjusting to the changes in her life. Victoria was left with a billion-dollar company that had been in her family for generations. Being a CEO would have been a challenge for any twenty-year old lady. But with the help of her staff, Victoria became an effective manager of the company.

She walked to the pool area and looked into the water's surface that reflected so many images and shades of light. Hidden below was a force of destruction. Victoria always considered drowning to be the worst way to die. She owned an Olympic pool but could not swim. There was something about large bodies of water that presented a fear she could not overcome.

Victoria believed that people's emotions and passions were presented in different shades of color. She believed that each color spoke a hidden language that only she understood. Red was depicted as compassionate and fiery, meaning that you were someone who loved hard. Blue was the spirit color that represented desire, the will to be relentless and determined. The vibrations of black conversed with the grays and browns, sent messages to the yellow horizons. Pink was her favorite. She found pink to be the shade of valor and wisdom.

For Victoria, life was an anomaly, an absurdity that locked away the meaning of her existence. Her purpose was often-times altered by her current state of mind. She sat on the edge of the marble bathtub and ran her hands through the water. "I can see you," she said to the image reflected in the water's surface. It was perplexing how she could stare at an image in the mirror and not recognize it. The eyes, the high cheek bones, and pink lips appeared to be of another. Victoria stood and walked to the full-length mirror and removed her robe and examined the appearance of her naked body; honey-colored with a hint of caramel; blemish free and flawless. Victoria ran her fingers through the long, jet-black hair that hung well below her shoulders. She noticed that her breasts had nipples the size of quarters and were sensitive to the touch.

Victoria stepped into the bathtub filled with water, submerged herself and opened her eyes. It seemed so quiet and peaceful. But when she began to come up for air, her body was unable to move. Something or someone did not allow her to surface. Panic and her desperation for air, caused her lungs to take in water. Victoria then bolted from underneath the water and held onto the tub's edge, fearing that someone would pull her back under. She wiped at her face while catching her breath. She was locked inside an imaginary prison fashioned by her thoughts and expedited by her worst fears.

* * *

The rainstorm was violent and showed no sign of subsiding. The winds roared and shook the windowpanes, while the lightning and thunder added chaos to the existing storm. The power had been knocked out and the backup generator had not kicked in. Victoria's room was pitch black and filled with an eerie darkness that would scare any ten-year old girl. Victoria hid underneath blankets and sheets, creating her private sanctuary.

"Please go away, please go away, please go away," Victoria repeated, hoping that the storm would hear her plea. She then heard the sound of the door opening into her room. Her heart pounded with fear. She relaxed and smiled as her mother looked under the covers and joined her.

"Hey you. What are you doing under here?"

"The rain and thunder scared me," Victoria replied as her voice trembled with fear.

"I'll protect you and beat the storm up if it bothers you again," her mother said.

She looked into her daughter's eyes, recognizing the purity and innocence of a harmless child. Victoria was the joy and purpose of Lana's life.

"But if the lightning strikes you, I thought that it would hurt really bad," Victoria questioned.

"Well it can hurt people, but not you. You're too precious and the lightning knows better than to mess around with me," Lana said as she touched the tip of her daughter's shiny nose.

"You know what I think? We should get a closer look at the storm. You'll see that it isn't something to be afraid of," Lana said.

Victoria reacted with an expression of fear. But before she knew it, Lana had moved her to the window and pulled the curtains back. The rain continued to pour as the lightning and thunder caused Victoria to jerk back in fear.

"Look Victoria," her mother said. "The rain is the world's way of crying when it is sad. Thunder and lightning protect the rain like I guard you."

Victoria looked at the dark sky and for the first time in her life, she wasn't afraid. A bolt of lightning caught her eye. It was beautiful, she thought. The color projected was astonishing. Victoria walked closer to the window and put her hand on the glass, feeling the vibrations as the thunder roared. The storm cried out to her. There was nothing to fear.

"I'm sorry you're sad," Victoria whispered to the storm. Lana smiled at her daughter's courage.

"You want to go and take a closer look?" Victoria nodded yes. When they made it to the front door, Lana opened it. The gusting winds nearly blew Victoria back inside the house. Victoria laughed as she followed her mother onto the porch. The two of them ran into the rain as if there were no worries. Lana fell into the grass where Victoria joined her.

"Come and play with us, Mr. Butler," Lana yelled.

"That's alright. I'll wait here," he replied as he stood holding dry towels for the two of them.

Victoria woke from her dream and stared at the ceiling. Lately, she'd been dreaming a lot about her mother. Mourning Lana's death had become her permanent reality. Having said that, Victoria knew that she had to find a purpose for living and not allow the sadness to consume her.

CHAPTER THREE

Chanel

Someone knocked on the door. Chanel slowly awakened as her head seemed to explode from a massive migraine. Her head spun for a few seconds before she managed to focus her eyes and realize that she was in a hotel room. Chanel's drug highs were usually followed by a brief struggle to recall events that she had experienced. But this time seemed worse than before.

The hotel manager and housekeeping entered Chanel's room and found her struggling to stand. "Are you okay?" the manager asked. "Do you need a doctor?"

"No, I'm fine."

"It's check-out time and the room needs to be serviced. You have to leave." Chanel waved the manager off as she began to gather her things. She then walked into the bathroom and caught a glimpse of herself in the mirror. She looked tired and her makeup was smeared across her face; eyes appeared dilated and lifeless; and she seemed to have aged overnight.

Chanel made it to her car, taking a moment to gather her thoughts. She turned the ignition on, but the car wouldn't start. She repeated the process a few times before realizing that the gas gauge was on empty. "Great, just fucking great," Chanel yelled as she rested her head on the steering wheel. The only gas station was about a mile down the road. She looked into the rearview mirror and salvaged what she could of her appearance.

Chanel took small strides as she labored to walk in a pair of high heels. Out of desperation, she removed the shoes and finished the walk in bare feet. Except for a young clerk, the gas station was empty. Chanel then realized that she had left her purse in the car. What can happen next, she thought.

"Can I help you?" the clerk asked.

"I actually came for some gas, but I left my wallet in the car," Chanel explained. "If you can allow me to get a gas can and some gas, I will be right back to pay you. I'll give you something extra for your troubles."

"I'm sorry, but I would lose my job if I gave you free gas," the clerk explained.

"I just need to take some gas back to my car where my wallet is. I will pay you then."

"I'm sorry. I can't do it," the clerk replied. Chanel noticed that the clerk could not keep his eyes off her breasts that seemed to jump out of her bra. She then turned on her charm and did the thing that she does best.

"What's your name if you don't mind me asking?"

"My name is Coby, but everybody calls me TJ." It was obvious that he was nervous as Chanel leaned over the counter giving him a better look at her breasts.

"I don't want to get you fired. It looks like you enjoy your job. So what do you say if I do something for you and in return, you pay for my gas? It will be a win-win. Both of us will get something we want."

"What kind of deal are you talking about?" the clerk asked as his face blushed.

Chanel was losing her patience and got to the point. "What do you say? I'll suck your dick and you give me a can of gas and a ride to my car."

"I can't leave the store," he replied.

Chanel was becoming impatient. "Do you want the blow job or not?"

The clerk looked around thinking that someone might be watching. He then leaned forward and told her to go to the back near the coolers.

Minutes later Chanel was walking down the road carrying a gas can with her high heels swung around her shoulders.

* * *

The wind blew through her hair as she raced through traffic in her convertible. Chanel was drawn to dangerous activities and speeding down the highway was one of them. While Chanel didn't consider herself to be an escort, she had several men for clients.

Chanel's phone rang. "Gerald Day. I haven't heard from you in quite some time. How are you doing?" Gerald was rich beyond your imagination. He and Chanel were what you might consider to be opposites. While Gerald was in his 70s and Chanel was barely 20, the sexual attraction to Gerald was not an issue.

"I was out of the country on business and couldn't get away, which is part of the reason for me calling you. Would you accompany me on a trip to Canada? I have an event with some of my friends and would like for you to accompany me," Gerald explained.

"Of course, darling. I would never deny the great Mr. Gerald Day," she replied in her best prestigious dialogue. "Just text me the particulars and where to be. Will I need a passport?"

"No, not at all. My private jet gets access through Coin Development with their government. We'll be alright," Gerald said, leaving Chanel with no idea what he was talking about. Gerald was always a good time and his parties were always lavish. He was amongst the one-percent wealthiest people in the world.

"I'll see you later doll, take care," he said as he ended the call.

While at a stop light, she opened her purse and pulled out a small bag filled with a white powdery substance. She dug her fingernail into the bag and sniffed the powder into her nose. Chanel enjoyed snorting Coke, but she loved heroin. Cocaine was the gateway drug that preceded the ultimate high — heroin. Chanel started her car and sped through rush-hour traffic without a care in the world.

Chanel was involved in an auto accident a few months ago leaving someone severely injured. The courts found her partially responsible and gave her one-year probation and one-hundred hours of one-on-one talk therapy with a phycologist. Chanel believed that her psychologist, Dr. Smith, to be passionate about her job and overly assertive. When Chanel entered Dr. Smith's office, she quickly became comfortable as she sat in a stuffed, leather recliner. Of course it didn't hurt that she was high from an earlier snort of Coke. Being that Smith was in her early thirties, she was able to relate to some of Chanel's problems.

"How are you feeling today Ms. Rosenthal?"

"I'm fine. Just floating on a cloud as usual."

"In our last session we were talking about locating the center of your problems and learning how to shut them off. Have you been focusing on the assignments that I've suggested?"

"Not really. I don't think that my issues can be removed from my life," Chanel replied. The fact that Chanel was brutally honest served as an asset to therapy. While some of the things that she shared were a bit detailed and graphic, it was her truth to tell in any form she deemed fit.

"You told me once that your father was the reason that you don't trust men. Is that what brought about the promiscuity?"

"I wouldn't say so. But I think it made it easier for me to control them. Over time, some even became enjoyable. Most of them, if not all, are married men. They're just looking for a good time, and that's what I offer without complaint. I do what they want me to do and I act out fantasies."

"And what do you get in return?"

"I get what I need," Chanel answered.

"And what might that be?"

"Besides the money, I get to feel like I'm in charge. I'm given a purpose. To have that kind of control over men who are rich and powerful is exhilarating. Every woman wants to feel appreciated and they do that for me," Chanel explained. She closed her eyes and became lost in the moment.

"Tell me about some of these men," Smith asked.

"What do you want to know?"

"How do they fulfill your needs? I want to know how they make you feel."

"Are you sure you're ready for that conversation Doc? I wouldn't want to get you all hot and bothered."

"This isn't about me. I'll be fine," Smith assured her.

"The one that I have in mind, I'll just call him Bobby. He's different than most of my male clients. He's more attentive and in tune with how my body works. Sometimes I'm tempted to call him on the days when I feel the urge to be held, to be treated with compassion, and touched with fondness." Chanel was getting so caught up in the moment that her legs parted while she rubbed her calf along the side of the recliner. Her hands began to rub the fabric between her legs, causing the friction to stimulate an arousal. Dr. Smith watched her and for a second she stopped writing and gave Chanel her undivided attention.

"Does this make you feel as if you need this sense of enchantment over men?"

"Sometimes I do, and other times I feel more dependent on drugs. That gives me a different kind of high than pleasure. Heroin makes me feel accepted and in control, permitting the level of high that I need. The thrill and excitement it brings is just indescribable. Sex is like having sex. But drugs are like making love. It's slow and sensual, passionate and in control," Chanel explained.

"What do you think, Doc? You think I'm screwed up?"

"I think you are searching for something that you have to figure out before it gets away from you. I look at you and see a beautiful young woman. I think you have some things to sort out," Smith said.

Chanel turned to face her. "I lost my virginity to a man who took advantage of me, more than once. Drugs only helped later, but before that I was forced to endure the pain and discomfort. I appreciate what life has taught me, but I'll never forget what it put me through," Chanel explained.

"Why do you allow your past to have so much control over you? Most people don't forget, but they manage to move on. It's as if you're weaponizing your rationale to justify your actions. This is what we call self-destructive behavior," Smith added.

"Have you ever been raped?" Chanel asked, knowing that her question caught Smith off guard.

Smith gathered her thoughts. "No, I haven't."

"Well, I have. More times than I can remember. Life made me angry and violent. So having a temporary escape is the only way most people can cope. This is how I deal with the things I've been through."

"With sex and drugs?"

"Not so much on sex, but yes on drugs. Sex is just the opening act for a great show. I'm more addicted to the control aspect of creating orgasms perfected through the art of self-reliance. And having the ability to control bodies with the sway of my hips or the squinting of my eyes," Chanel explained as she shared a slight smile.

"I think that you are in tune with yourself which is a great thing. I just think you're using it for all of the wrong reasons. What are you good at? What's your passion, your talents?"

"I love the water. I love to swim and be in the open waters. There's something about it that's soothing."

"Maybe you should try to swim whenever you feel the need for sex or drugs."

"Once you've used sex and drugs to cope, there's nothing else in this world that could replace them," Chanel admitted.

"I know a good friend who runs a swim class throughout the week. But on weekends, it's open swim. She wouldn't mind if I sent you there to use the pools. I swim there myself as a stress reliever. I think that you should consider it. At least give it a try, and if you don't like it you don't have to commit to it. In fact, I'll count it towards your counseling hours."

"Are you trying to save me Doc?"

"Saving isn't the word I'd use. I'm trying to get you to find what it is that you're looking for."

"Maybe I've already found it and I'm bored of it already," Chanel said as she stood to leave. But not before Smith asked one more questions

"Before you can go I want to ask you one last question."

"You're the shrink."

"You never told me what your father did that was so bad."

"He was the man that raped me."

CHAPTER FOUR

Victoria

While Victoria was not anxious to attend the masquerade, she would do anything to protect her mother's name. If Lana had attended these events, so would Victoria. Lana liked the attention and enjoyed having Bloom as her last name. Lana's parents had left her the mining companies, and now Lana passed the inheritance to Victoria.

The Bloom Mining Company began many years ago through the efforts of Victoria's great, great grandparents. While others combed the African continent looking for gold and precious jewels, the Blooms turned their attention to Winnipeg, Canada. It should be added that other entrepreneurs thought the Blooms were crazy for ignoring the African mines. It was through the old rock and coal mines where the Blooms looked for their first discovery. But they had found nothing and were about to call it quits.

By hanging on for a few more months, their luck changed. Her great grandparents discovered rare gems and other stones in mountains laced with gold. The Blooms eventually purchased all of the land that the mountains sat on and expanded their discoveries by leasing out portions of it to other companies. They had created a fortune that was passed on from one generation to the next.

Victoria's car pulled up to the ball room where the masquerade was being held. Many people stood outside hoping to be seen by the flashing cameras and to see who would win this year's stylish entry. There were also the elderly men flaunting young women 30 plus years their junior.

Some people considered these events to be repulsive and filled with egotistical maniacs. But the beautiful thing about masquerades was the fact that you could hide behind your mask. Victoria didn't plan on staying long; just long enough to give her respects on behalf of her mother. Victoria's hair had a natural look as it was long and reached down her back. She wore an Alexander McQueen pencil dress and couldn't resist showing off her mother's fifty carat tennis necklace. Not because she wanted to make a statement, it was more out of respect for something that Lana would have worn.

Inside the venue were servers on both levels pushing drinks to the guests. Victoria took a champagne flute and stood in a corner hoping not to draw attention. She believed the world of the rich and famous were all about politics. Who you knew and how you became a guest were everything. As she sat back and surveyed the room, someone tapped her on the shoulder.

"Ms. Bloom, I'm glad you were able to make it. It's an honor to have you in attendance. Your mother was an exquisite woman," the elderly man said.

"Thank you," Victoria replied. But to her surprise, the man raised his flute of champagne and began tapping it with a fork.

"Excuse me everyone. This is the daughter of Elana Bloom. I would like for you to make her feel at home." People began bombarding her with introductions and telling her about their relationship with Elana. This was a lot for Victoria to absorb. She soon made an excuse and headed to the ladies' bathroom; locked the door and leaned against it. She then tugged at the top of dress, hoping to gain her breath.

"It's that bad out there, huh?" A voice behind her asked. Victoria quickly turned and saw this beautiful woman with long, dark hair and blemish-free skin. The woman sat on the window ledge and lit a cigarette.

"I don't like being asked too many questions, especially by a group of strangers," Victoria explained.

"My name is Chanel. You are?"

"I'm Victoria."

"I guess your date forgot to warn you about the attention. Old rich-men can be relentless."

"Date, I don't understand." Victoria was confused.

"Date, as in the gentleman that brought you here," Chanel clarified. She had assumed that Victoria was just someone's show piece because she was the youngest woman there and given her age, she probably wasn't rich.

"No, I don't have a date. I actually came alone," Victoria answered.

Chanel was confused. "So, how did you get into this event? Why are you here?" Chanel asked.

"This stupid honorary guess list that my mother was on. She passed so I took her place," Victoria explained.

Chanel knew all about the event because her date, Gerald, told her the specifics. "So you're a rich girl?"

"If that's how you want to put it," Victoria replied.

"If you don't mind, how old are you?" Chanel asked.

"I'm twenty. My birthday is next month."

"What's your last name," Chanel asked.

"Bloom. Victoria Bloom."

Chanel googled her name and a bunch of information popped up, including what she was worth. "Damn girl. Your worth more money than you'll ever be able to spend in a lifetime."

"Money isn't everything," Victoria shared.

"I can agree with you on that," Chanel said. "I have to go. It was nice meeting you," Chanel said as she left the rest room.

There was something about her that seemed familiar, Victoria thought. Perhaps it was her composure that gained Victoria's attention. She then noticed a shiny object on the floor and reached down to pick it up. It was jewelry in the shape of a dolphin. She quickly left the rest room to find Chanel and return the dolphin. Chanel was gone.

* * *

Victoria's long ride home had a Zen-like quality to it. She enjoyed listening to music, reading, nature walks and yearning to be the free spirited woman her mother had raised her to be. But somehow, that wasn't her reality. While she met with many people on a daily basis, she seemed isolated from the world. The loneliness contributed to a life void of social interactions with other people. This was the side of Victoria that most people never knew. After all, with this much wealth how could she not be happy?

Lana was a good entertainer, the life of the party some might say. Her enthusiasm was infectious. She took charge and commanded attention; all traits that Victoria admired. When Victoria was a little girl, Lana told her stories about a magical river that was similar to a wishing well. But instead of tossing coins into it, you meditated over the desires and passions you hoped to have. The river was to be your moral compass, leading you to peace and tranquility.

Victoria loved hearing stories about the magical river that her mother told her each night before going to sleep. As the years passed, so did the stories of true love and happiness. Victoria now realized that she was young and naive to have believed in such things.

It never dawned on Victoria that her mother wasn't happy or her relentless pursuit for love had not been fulfilled. While Lana had her share of lovers, the relationships were short lived. Lana was good at hiding her secrets, appearing to always be in control. But Victoria loved her even if it was just the two of them. When Lana died, the doctor said it was from a heart attack. But Victoria knew better. Perhaps her mother died of a broken heart.

Victoria looked aimlessly out the car window as they drove down the road. She was always looking for places to hide; anything that kept her from thinking about her loneliness. Her hand reached into the purse and pulled out the shiny dolphin that Chanel had dropped in the rest room. While it reminded Victoria of something, she couldn't remember what it was.

Light rain fell from the sky. Dark clouds suggested that a storm was close. Victoria smiled and put her hand on the window. The rain picked up rather quickly as the thunder emitted a recognizable growl.

Streaky bolts of lightning danced in the sky. "I'm sorry you're sad," Victoria whispered to the sky. This reminded Victoria how she loved the rainstorms, a constant reminder of Victoria and her mother running around and playing in the rain.

"Would you like for me to stop near the lake Ms. Bloom?" Mr. Butler inquired. He knew her well and how important it was for her to find moments of reflection.

"Yes, please," Victoria answered.

Mr. Butler pulled over and opened the car door for Victoria. The umbrella took a beating from the heavy rain. "When I was a little girl rainstorms used to scare me. I thought that thunder and lightning were the scariest thing on the face of the earth. But I was wrong. My mother taught me to see past the surface and appreciate the true beauty of the rainstorm."

"Oh I remember," Mr. Butler answered. "I declined all of your offers to join the two of you."

Victoria smiled and stepped from underneath the umbrella and walked towards the shoreline. She was soaked by rain as her hair fell down her back and the red dress morphed into a maroon mess. Victoria stretched her arms out and looked up into the sky. She then opened her mouth and let the raindrops hit her tongue. While Victoria was hurting on the inside, Mr. Butler enjoyed watching her have fun even if it was short lived.

Victoria had taken a hot bath and retired to her massive canopy bed. Her room's ceiling was a display of clouds, birds, and rain drops. Multiple paintings adorned the walls, some painted by Victoria and others by Lana. There were two skylights above her bed, allowing her to see the stars at night. She then thought about Chanel, the mystery girl from the masquerade party. Victoria was taken by Chanel's energy and spirit and sensed a feeling that the two of them had known each other in an earlier life. It was a feeling that was not easily discarded.

Victoria wanted to find Chanel and return the dolphin. Was it more than that? If so, what? She didn't know. But how could she find Chanel? Finding the person that brought her to the party would help. And if she did find Chanel, would she think that Victoria was stalking her? So many thoughts were racing through Victoria's mind. Perhaps I should stop my concerns over this lady called Chanel, Victoria thought.

Victoria thought about Lana and what she wanted Victoria to do with her life. It wasn't like Victoria had to be hands on with the company. She had a board and a management team capable of overseeing the daily operations. There was no need for her being there 100% of the time. Her primary purpose was to establish some goals and direction in her life.

CHAPTER FIVE

Chanel

I was in a day-dream state of mind. The heroin injected into my veins was followed by an unrestrained high, signaling that my self-induced high had begun. It's such a beautiful experience when my body becomes a mere feather floating in the clouds; allowing each sensual touch to activate my passion. Heroin is my lover.

Heroin kisses my neck and fondles my breasts as my nipples anticipate the wave of satisfaction to come. While I'm overcome with passion and filled with love, heroin conquers my mind, body, and soul. When without, I rage for my lover to flow through my veins again.

* * *

"Chanel, you're bleeding," said Jasmine, her best friend since childhood. The two of them had lived in the same neighborhood and were inseparable. Jasmine was Chanel's other half; someone who understood her like no other.

They were in the eighth grade when they slipped into her mother's bedroom to steal some prescription medication. "I had no idea what they were. I can only imagine that they were some kind of pain pills that my mother was taking for her broken arm. Anyway, that was our first high," Chanel explained.

Shortly after that experience, Chanel and Jasmine began smoking marijuana and drinking alcohol with high school students. Their experimentation grew into multiple drug-use accompanied by alcohol to carry them into their next high. "Jasmine was my ride or die, and I loved her very much," Chanel added. While the two of us did a lot of shit, we kept each other grounded no matter what.

Jasmine had long, jet-black hair that accented her youthful appearance; black eyes that demanded attention; and full lips begged to be kissed. And then there was her honey-gold complexion and vibrant personality.

"Your nose is bleeding." Jasmine repeated.

The two of them had too much alcohol and empty syringes. Chanel wiped at her nose with her shirt and saw more blood. She then removed her shirt and cleaned her nose. Although she had no recollection of making it back to the room, that was normal.

"I'm hot. I need some air," Chanel said as she went to the bathroom to rinse herself off and run cold water over her face. She dried herself and tried to make out the image in the mirror. The reflection staring back at Chanel seemed puzzling. The eyes appeared to be those of an older woman; the cheekbones had morphed into an unusual structure; and her appearance had taken on a different persona.

"You look like shit," Jasmine said as she pulled her panties down to use the toilet.

"Yeah, thanks for reminding me," Chanel replied. "Thanks for taking care of me. I don't remember a thing." While having Jasmine take care of her was common, something seemed different this time. But she didn't know what.

"You know I'll forever have your back, Baby Doll," Jasmine said. "I chipped a nail carrying you to the elevator and getting you to the room. If I don't take care of you, who will?"

Both Chanel and Jasmine made it to the bed and collapsed underneath a huge comforter. Chills ran through Chanel's body. She cycled from hot to cold and back again. By now, the high was subsiding and the fall from the top wasn't as inviting as the ascension to the top.

Chanel felt a massive migraine coming on, the one thing she dreaded the most when she returned to her drug-free normalcy.

Chanel's mind focused on the emptiness that was in her head. Life was like a crazy dream repeating over and over. Chanel was the star and the only one in it. Chanel knew she had to stop this vicious cycle, but how could she? She closed her eyes as the room began to spin. She grabbed hold of the bed and allowed herself to be swept up in a typhoon of dizziness. Chanel's adrenaline was through the roof and her heart pounded hard. She closed her eyes as she continued the ride.

Chanel gripped the sheets hard, hoping to find relief from the pain that consumed her. There was no oxygen in her lungs as she struggled for a final breath. She entered a full panic state, and then, without notice, it stopped. She opened her eyes and took a deep breath. A light breeze came through the window like a breath of fresh air. Jasmine had no idea that Chanel was on the brink of the devil's underground world called hell.

The two of them were a ball of chaos lacking any positive direction of where they might go. There were moments of silence when neither spoke. While Jasmine was in deep thought, Chanel wanted to figure her shit out and see where her life was headed.

"I think I want to go back to college and finish this time," Jasmine said. Jasmine was an intelligent woman, so it wasn't as if she couldn't succeed academically if that's what she chose to do. But Jasmine seemed to be in a different mental state, not ready for an educational setting.

"You're serious?" inquired Chanel.

"Girl, fuck no," Jasmine said. "I can't pass an exam if my life depended on it." Chanel joined Jasmine as they both fell over in laughter. "You know something?" Jasmine asked. "I'm glad we're still able to keep each other happy after all of these years. Some nights when I feel the worst, you keep a smile on my face."

"We work for each other and I'll forever have your back," Chanel replied. "But we do need to get our shit together." They continued their conversation throughout the night until they fell asleep.

* * *

Chanel was about to have another session with her court-appointed psychologist. She entered Dr. Smith's office and sat in the familiar recliner. Chanel did not hesitant to share her feelings with Dr. Smith. She loved the give and take between the two of them. The sessions addressed feelings that no medication could accomplish. The well-defined details of her sex life, the parties, drugs and nightlife were fair-game. Smith knew things about Chanel that Jasmine didn't know.

Chanel believed that Smith could be trusted, and that her demeanor was inviting. But at the end of the day, Chanel believed that the control was in her hands. Smith only knew what Chanel told her. In Chanel's mind, the narrator has the flexibility to narrate a truth or a lie, and maybe both. No one would know the difference, and that's what Chanel found to be intriguing.

The world is filled with so many mysteries, leaving us access to what our mind accepts as reality. Do we really know those close to us? Lies are a powerful deception. Dr. Smith was a pawn in Chanel's game of chess that was about to begin. But Dr. Smith was game and was familiar with the rules.

Chanel was sitting near the window looking down from the 16th floor. "Have you ever had a patient who tried to jump from this window?" Chanel asked.

"I don't deal with suicidal cases, just those who need someone to talk to."

"Most suicidal cases start that way," Chanel surmised. "You never know who has the tendency to kill themselves until it happens. How do you know that I'm not suicidal?"

"I don't know. Are you?"

"Not today," Chanel answered as she headed back to the recliner.

"How are you feeling today?" Smith asked.

"I really don't know how to answer that question. The day just started for me."

"I see that you're all dressed up. What's the occasion?" Smith asked.

Chanel had on a white dress with fire-red heels. Her hair was gathered into a bun and her lips sported a deep, red color. Chanel's taste was simple, yet elegant.

"I'm still filling out my day," Chanel responded. "I plan on having an eventful night, so why not dress for the occasion?"

The psychologist knew that Chanel was a bit of a wild card, and never sure what she might share. "I consider you to be a free spirit, sexually open so to speak. Do you feel there's a reason you're so, I'm trying to find the right word, promiscuous?"

Chanel interrupted. "Yes, for the lack of a better word. I'm a woman who chooses to be sexually liberated and pleasing. And I don't think that's a problem."

"I think you have a disconnection with your childhood."

"Maybe, maybe not. What are you getting at?" Chanel asked.

"I think your disregard for men is due to the lack of not having a father in your life, or being hurt by a man you trusted," Dr. Smith replied.

"Life can be complicated," Chanel stated with a slight smile.

"If I'm wrong about anything, just voice your objections. I'm only responding to the things you've told me during past sessions," the psychologist explained.

"I never had a father, so I can't speak in terms of my actions due to a void that has never been filled." Chanel's voice became tense.

"Has there ever been any role models in your life that were male?"

"What does that have to do with anything?" Chanel was becoming agitated and her body posture had shifted. Smith knew that she had struck a nerve.

"I'm just trying to identify your reasoning. Nothing more," Smith explained.

"My Uncle Terry. That's all I'm willing to share about him. Don't ask me questions about him," Chanel demanded.

"That's fair," Smith responded. "Do you think had your father been around, things would have been a lot different?"

"I can't say yes, and I can't say no because I've never had a father," Chanel explained.

Dr. Smith decided to redirect the same question. "Would you say your consideration of men is due to the lack of a father not being in your life?"

While the psychologist posed her question, Chanel did not immediately respond. Instead, she allowed her thoughts to settle in. One thing was certain. Chanel hated to appear vulnerable and lose control of her emotions. It was obvious that Chanel was holding back. It was Smith's job to pinpoint the trigger that brought on her reaction. Smith was aware of the fact that control was the big issue for Chanel.

"Men are creatures of habit, aroused by beauty and filled with ego," Chanel explained. "They have this fantasy of being pleased by the very things that are beyond their grasp. Things that they could never achieve. The absence of my father has nothing to do with my relationship with men. I choose to have control over both my desires and theirs."

"Wouldn't you consider that to be internal damage from the years of your adolescence? The pain and suffering you've been subjected to," Smith inquired.

"We're all damaged one way or the other," Chanel answered. "There's a repeating cycle that'll forever keep us in a continuous loop. We all use each other for our selfish reasons, and that's just the reality of it. Men use women all the time and their actions are often deemed as some noble gesture. But when women do the same, we're looked down upon, and labeled as a deviate, a scarlet woman even. I choose to be bold and callous of what other people say about me."

There was a look in Chanel's eyes that her psychologist interpreted as the truth. Chanel was telling the truth and being true to what she believed. The psychologist deemed her to be an extreme case; one she found to be intriguing. There was something about Chanel that Smith couldn't quite wrap her finger around. But Chanel was worth her time for sure.

Chanel was highly educated, beautiful, and filled with so much life. So much so that most people wondered why she wasn't married and climbing to the top of her chosen profession. "Women are judged by different standards. I find it a bit intrusive, but that's just the way society works. It's my understanding that you suffered abuse from older men as a child. Correct?" asked Dr. Smith.

"My actions aren't driven from my past and insinuating so shows that you aren't listening," Chanel hurled her reply. "My past is buried, and I care nothing about revisiting it."

"I think you're unaware of how disconnected you are from your past. I feel as if you have unresolved issues and you're unresponsive to the issue at hand." Smith said as she wrote a few notes in her folder. As she continued to talk, Chanel's mind drifted to an earlier time in her life.

THE PAST, WHEN CHANEL
WAS NINE-YEARS OLD...

As a child, I was unaware of the silent dangers that lurked about in the darkest nights. My reality was a blueprint offered by role models who determined what I was allowed to see and hear. While I was encased in an imaginary cocoon designed to protect me from predators, that was not always the case.

One night changed everything. The memories are locked into my head and are seemingly part of my DNA. I never knew my biological father and was clueless as to why he wasn't around. Uncle Terry, my mother's kid brother, was the closest thing to a father that I had ever known. I loved Terry.

At the time, we lived in an old house that I swear was as alive as any person I knew. The house spoke its own language through the creaking hardwood floors; the age-old plumbing; the screeching sounds of closing doors; and the howling that the chimney regurgitated throughout the night. To cope with the house that spoke, I created a make-shift tent out of sheets and blankets. This was my sanctuary, the place where I felt safe, the place where I prayed for the house not to speak.

On this night, a thunderstorm knocked out the power leaving the house in complete darkness with only my flashlight for protection. Tree branches banged against the house while lighting followed the paralyzing sound of thunder.

There was movement on the side of my bed as if someone was about to threaten my sanctuary. My first thought was to jump from the tent and make a run for it, but my legs were unable to move. Then, Uncle Terry appeared. As he lifted my blanket, I let out a sigh of relief. I smiled as he entered my tent.

"Why are you still up?" Terry asked.

"The house and storm are making scary sounds."

"You don't have to be afraid of this old house. You know that I would never let anything bad happen to you," Uncle Terry explained as he slid under my covers. At the time, it felt okay. After all, it was Uncle Terry. But when you're a child, your mind doesn't process behavior beyond your barriers of innocence.

"Come here," Uncle Terry said as he pulled me closer and squeezed me tight. Even then, I thought this to be a bit puzzling. He then kissed my neck and pressed his wet lips against mine, allowing me no chance of pulling away. My heart pounded and my mind tried to escape the horror being inflicted upon me. I had moved from being happy to see Uncle Terry, to being petrified of him. He forced my lips apart, sliding his slobbering tongue deep into my mouth. He reached under my night grown and touched my forbidden place. I shivered as my soul began to die.

"Chanel, Chanel! Are you listening to me?" Dr. Smith asked as she tried to regain her attention. A tear escaped Chanel's eye as she wiped at it. While Smith noticed the change in Chanel's demeanor, she hesitated to ask why Chanel was crying. After all, she would probably make something up or refuse to answer the question.

"I'm sorry, what were you saying?" Chanel asked as she struggled to shut down the memory that brought her pain.

"I know we're not supposed to touch issues not outlined in our agreement for treatment, but we need to discuss something from your past. It's all connected to who you are today. What were you thinking about before I brought you back to our conversation? It seemed to be quite hurtful." Smith considered this to be a critical point in the therapy.

"Something that'll never leave my head," Chanel replied. "No matter how hard I try to bury it, it always finds a way to resurface."

"That's because it's an unresolved issue. You'll never be free until you deal with it. The pain you feel is connected to your past. If you continue to harbor these things, it'll do you more harm," Smith explained.

Chanel was stubborn and she knew that about herself, but it was a hurdle she had to clear. The only way Smith could help this young woman was to free her from the past.

I knew she was only trying to help me, but I didn't want it this way, Chanel thought. I just needed someone to talk to be reminded of the world's cruelty; the scars, both physical and mental, that are left from the battles I've endured.

*   *   *

I dance along the shadows of death
as if nothing else matters.
Dancing as death calls my name,
waiting for me to answer
and bare it's chains.
Drift into emptiness and lose me,
things I've never known before.

I dance along the shadows of death
as if nothing else matters.
Faded crimson days that pass me by.
Waiting for death as I begin to weep,
cradled in arms that rock me asleep.
Drifting into the depths of the ocean,
for those who dance along the shadows of death.

CHAPTER SIX

Victoria

Victoria walked into her office and was immediately surrounded by her secretary and company manager. Victoria had recently launched a company that drew in more business than anticipated. Her billion-dollar company, Bloom Capital, had enough capital to gain leverage when needed.

"How are you doing Ms. Bloom?" her secretary asked. "You have two meetings scheduled for this week; one in the states and the other in Germany."

"Please call me Victoria. Cancel the Germany trip. I won't be able to make it. I have other commitments."

"Will do, Ms. Bloom. I'm sorry. I mean Victoria. I'm just trying to make a good impression. I really need this job and I want to be respectful," Valerie, admitted.

Victoria didn't immediately reply. Instead, she studied the young woman who had to be no older than herself. "Where are you from Valerie?"

"Toronto, I'm from Toronto." Victoria could see that Valerie was nervous. It could be seen in her body language.

"You have nothing to worry about. Be yourself and you'll do just fine," Victoria said. And with that, Valerie left the office feeling quite happy.

Jason was the company manager and had been Victoria's childhood friend. Kap capital was a large trading company owned by Jason's family that found themselves in financial ruins. Victoria bought them out and kept Jason on because he knew how the company operated.

"You really dislike John Walsh that much?" Jason asked.

"Even if I didn't, flying all the way to Germany is unnecessary. He's asking for my capital after all, not the other way around," Victoria answered. "John Walsh is not my kind of guy."

"I think we have a good thing going here." Jason was always flirting with Victoria. There was no secret that he'd had a crush on her since their adolescence. Victoria never considered Jason in a romantic way and considered him more like a brother.

"What do you think about the trip to California?" Victoria inquired.

"I think it's necessary. We're establishing an office there. You can't hide yourself in Canada forever. Eventually the world will put a face to the name," Jason explained.

"I guess you're right. I just hate flying."

"Then why do you own a slew of private jets?" Jason asked in a joking way.

"How soon are you flying out to California?" Victoria asked.

"As soon as possible. Have you ever been to the United States?"

"No, I have not," Victoria shot back.

"Then you're in for a treat."

*　*　*

The nights and days moved slow like mud on a rainy day; an indication of Victoria's boring and predictable life. Some people had a preconceived notion that wealth guaranteed happiness. But to Victoria, there was no connection between the two.

While Victoria's mother, Lana, shared many valuable lessons with her daughter, she sheltered her from what she perceived as the ugly nature of the world. In doing so, Lana's death freed Victoria from the imaginary prison that had been constructed for her. Now that the walls around her had fallen, the air held a different smell.

Victoria studied the stars through the sky light of her bedroom, fascinated by the stories they told. Often times, she closed her eyes and imagined herself flying through the endless sky filled with mysteries that Victoria would soon discover. She created images out of stars and gave them names. Sometimes they maintained their original shape; other times they came and went in unpredictable ways. Creativity had become her friend.

Now it was only Mr. Butler who had known Victoria since she made her entrance into the world. Mr. Butler, a soft-spoken man, was as gentle and kind as a butterfly. He understood Victoria and would protect her with his life.

It was late at night and Victoria couldn't sleep. She climbed out of bed and walked to the balcony. The cool, night wind cut through the fabric of her pajamas. She spread her arms as if she was flying while the wind blew through her long hair. Victoria yearned to discover her preordained purpose. Working helped her navigate through the boredom. Victoria's mother taught her to fend for herself and maintain a business-oriented mindset. Since the inheritance, Victoria had doubled her net-worth and her investments were quite lucrative.

Victoria left the balcony, walked into her office, and picked up the phone. After a few rings, Jason answered. It was obvious that he had been sleeping. "I think I want to buy a place in California," Victoria said.

"And you just suddenly came up with this thought?" Jason asked as he took a moment to look at the clock. "Two o'clock in the morning?" Jason's voice reflected an air of disbelief.

"I think it'll be a great move, and I'll have the opportunity to learn the ins-and-outs of the states." Victoria was excited.

"Jason, are you still there?" she asked.

"Unfortunately, I am."

"So, what do you think?"

"Normally people don't think this late, but you're the only person who operates during these hours. I think it's a great idea Victoria. Can I go back to sleep now? I'll make arrangements to have my realtor find some homes for view. I'll see you in a few hours."

Victoria ended the call with a smile on her face.

*   *   *

"You sent for me boss?" Valerie asked as she made her way through Victoria's office door.

"Just Victoria, you can call me Victoria. And yes, I sent for you. It's my understanding that before coming here, you attended college in the states, UCLA to be exact?"

"Yes, I was part of the student international exchange program. I attended UCLA for four years. But I eventually stayed in the states for a few years after doing numerous interns and other things related to trading stocks," Valerie explained.

Victoria paused as she processed Valerie's revelation. "You're fired," Victoria said. "Your service is no longer needed here."

"I'm sorry," Valerie said. "I can work harder. I really need this job." Valerie turned flush red and looked as if she was about to pass out.

"I need a personal assistant, and I think you'll fit the job quite well. Your pay will also be increased for accepting it on such a short notice," Victoria explained.

Valerie nearly passed out, followed by "I can do that. Thank you, thank you."

Jason walked into the office as Valerie shot pass him and almost knocked him to the floor.

"What's her deal?" Jason inquired.

"I fired her and hired her as my personal assistant."

"Good for her. I talked to a realtor and she faxed me a few homes on the market." Jake passed her a file. While Victoria looked over the information, she was not impressed.

"This shit looks like my grandmother picked them out for her retirement home." Victoria gave the file back to Jason. "How long would it take to have a place built from the ground up?"

"We'll have to meet with a designer, find the space we're looking at, maybe three to four years top," Jason explained.

Victoria had a look of defeat on her face. "Get the realtor on the phone."

Jason made the call and placed it on speaker. "Hello," a voice on the other end answered.

"Hi, my name is Victoria Bloom and I'm looking to purchase a home in your area."

"Okay. Do you have any idea what you're looking for?"

"Something young and vibrant. Space, lots of space," Victoria replied.

"And what's your budget?"

"I have no budget."

"Okay, that's good to know. And how soon are we talking?"

"Yesterday, as soon as possible," Victoria answered.

"Let me get back to you and we can go from there."

"That'll be fine," Victoria said as she ended the call and looked at Jason.

"What do you think about taking things over here for a while?"

"What do you mean a while?" Jason questioned.

"I don't know, maybe indefinitely. Who's to say. I want to get away from work for a while. After all, this is something you've wanted your entire life. Now you can make it a reality," Victoria explained.

"And you're ready to let it all go, just like that?"

"Jason, it's not like I can't afford to walk away from it all. We can crunch the numbers later and go from there. I just need to live my life for a change."

"And what will you do?"

"I don't know. Maybe get into film or just travel. I haven't got that far yet, but I'll figure it out," Victoria explained.

"If that's what you want to do, then I'll support you in any way I can. But what about me?" Jake asked.

"You won't miss me. I'll just be a phone call away. You'll live. I'm sure of it. Besides, you're the one I need to get away from," Victoria joked. "Now, out of my office. I need to make some calls."

Jason got up to leave, but not before giving her his final thought. "I'm going to miss you."

*   *   *

Our life experiences coupled with our DNA make us who we are today. Now that I'm older, I question who I am. I've been dictated to and led down a path of uncertainty. I'm grateful for the things that my mother left me; being in the upper one percent of society's wealth is a remarkable gift. Although our philosophy and moral compass didn't align, Lana was a woman that I admired.

"And if I may inquire, what adventures does this departure beckon?" Mr. Butler asked as Victoria was pulling out her luggage.

"I plan on taking a trip to California for a while. Will you miss me?"

"California is quite the distance from Yellow Knife, and if I may be frank, your absence will be missed a great deal."

"You're an adventurous man Mr. Butler. So, what do you suggest I get into?"

"Given the years I've invested with the Blooms, you women have a taste not suitable for anything less than ravishing. I feel that you will find your way without my guidance."

"Have you always been so wise?"

"For as long as the sky can turn blue." he joked. Mr. Butler left Victoria to the task at hand.

The United States was a nation to behold and Victoria knew that she was in for a ride. The mere uncertainty generated a feeling of excitement. She needed to do something for herself and step away from the life that Lana had created for her. It was time to write her own story.

Most people would be reluctant to travel down an unfamiliar path, but I was prepared to conquer the world. There wasn't an ounce of hesitation as I prepared for my trip to the United States. Maybe this time around I'll experience the things I was deprived of as a child. If things don't work out, I gave it my best shot.

CHAPTER SEVEN

Chanel

I cringed in both the satisfaction and pain as he entered me with his full length, stretching my vaginal walls further apart with each stroke. He dug deep into my stomach causing my body to react with each and every stride. It was sad how sexual gratification can take me to the highest points of euphoria, and then bring me crashing down once it's over. My body wanted him to dig deeper, but his penis wasn't large enough to hit the spots that I needed to be touched.

I began rubbing myself in unison as he held me. I bit down on my bottom lip and imagined that he was someone else, someone more attractive. I was good at pretending as I worked to please myself. I pinched my nipple with the other hand and felt myself beginning to cum. It was a feeling that I knew all too well. The moans that escaped my mouth were cries of pleasure. I started to ride him harder and thrust my hips into his body as if I nearly split myself in half. My nails dug deep into his chest, and the sweat from our bodies acted as a natural lubricant.

While I came so hard that my body was shaking, his audacity made me angry. He acted as he alone had brought me to the point of climax. But like I've said, I was good at pretending. It was not about him. He was merely a vessel being used for my pleasures. My juices ran down his sides as I slowly grinded on

top of him, allowing the complete wave of my orgasm to past.
My pussy was wet and filled with a thick white substance.

I got off of him and was ready to bring this ordeal to a close.
I skillfully took all of him into my mouth and swallowed him
whole. My tongue did tricks around the tip of his head as my
mouth was still shut.

I looked into his blue eyes and saw all the way to his soul.
I knew that I had defeated him in ways he'd never overcome.
He tried to challenge my gaze and regain his composure as if I
was just some chick he had called to treat himself. I held onto
my gaze as my tongue and lips worked in unison to break him.
I could tell that he wanted to look away so his true nature
wouldn't be exposed. But I already knew he was weak. These
are the men that I like to destroy. He turned away as his knees
buckled underneath me. I stood and walked to the shower
without speaking a word. Besides, what was there to say?

AN HOUR LATER:

"Let's get on the Ferris wheel," Jasmine suggested as they headed towards the ride. Jasmine and Chanel loved the carnival, especially the cotton candy. Jasmine climbed into the cart and waited for Chanel to join her. Although exhausted, there was no way that Chanel would deny Jasmine a night on the town. Chanel joined Jasmine on the Ferris wheel, grabbing hold of her as if they were two children sharing a joyful moment.

"Let's take a picture?" Jasmine yelled as she used her phone to take a selfie.

"You're just a ball of energy, aren't you?" Chanel asked with a smile on her face.

"I know what you need." Jasmine smiled as she removed a small capsule from her purse. She then placed the pill in Chanel's hand, making her swallow a *Molly*.

"That should do the trick in just a jiffy my baby doll." Chanel couldn't help but laugh. Jasmine was as high as a kite.

"You're a mess," Chanel said. When the ride ended Chanel wanted to get on the graviton. The line was wrapped around the barriers. They decided to duck under the ropes and butt the entire line. While some people objected, Chanel flipped them off and headed into the machine. Once they were positioned inside, there were two guys who tried to gain their attention.

"Excuse me, my name is..." One of the guys began to say as he was cut off by Jasmine.

"I'm not trying to be rude, but my friend just found out her boyfriend gave her aids. I'm just trying to cheer her up," Jasmine said. The look on his face was priceless.

"Why would you tell him that? You could have been the one with aids," Chanel joked.

When the ride spun in full force, Chanel felt the *Molly* kick in. Her heart pounded as she enjoyed the moment. Jasmine tried to move towards Chanel, but her body was stuck. Their eyes made contact as they blew kisses at each other. When the ride ended its twists and turns, Jasmine stumbled out of the machine and crashed to the ground in laughter. Chanel pulled Jasmine to her feet and the two of them marched to the food station.

"That was fun," Jasmine said. She turned her attention to the food-court worker. "You're cute," she said. His face blushed red. "What's your name?" Jasmine continued her charm.

"John, my name is John."

"Well, my name is Jasmine. Nice to meet you John."

"Do you have a girlfriend?" Chanel interjected.

"Um...yeah, I do," he replied as if he wanted to lie.

"Can I help you?" A young girl with pigtails approached and asked. You could tell that she felt threatened by the two beautiful vixens questioning her boyfriend.

"Yeah. I want a turkey leg and a pretzel," Jasmine said with a smile.

"And I'll have the same," Chanel added. The girl gave them a look that could kill and told John to get them their orders. Once John wrapped their food up and handed it to Jasmine, his girlfriend was still shooting daggers. Chanel and Jasmine looked at Jason.

"You have yourself a great night John, and if you find time to make your way to the parking lot, I'll suck your dick. We both will." While Jasmine walked off, you could hear his girlfriend screaming at him.

"You really would suck his dick?" Chanel asked.

"Sure, we both would," Jasmine answered as she took a bite of her turkey leg.

*   *   *

Chanel and Jasmine went to Jeff's condo. Not only was Jeff and Chanel friends, he was one of the largest heroin dealers in the area. Although Jeff was cool and down to earth, he was a heroin addict. He had a thing for Jasmine but never had the opportunity to share his feelings.

"So, what's up? You two look like you're blasted," Jeff said as he took a seat on the sofa.

"We each took a *Molly*, but the high is beginning to wear off. You know why we're here," Chanel said while taking some cash out of her purse.

"I'm out."

"You're lying. Why are you playing with me?" Chanel questioned.

"I'm serious. I'm out and my guy is out of town," Jeff answered.

Chanel had a look of disgust written on her face. "How the fuck do you call yourself a dope dealer and don't have any dope?" Chanel snapped.

"Yo, chill out. The shit don't just sit around and collect dust. I do have a stream of clientele. I can give my boy a call and have him get you straight."

"You're a real piece of shit, you know that?" Chanel vented. "Where the fuck is your guy?" she added.

"He'll come to us," Jeff replied.

"Call him up. But I'm telling you now, neither of us are fucking him," Chanel quickly added.

"And why would I think that?" Jeff shot back.

"Because most of you fuck heads think with your dicks when you see hot chicks," Chanel explained.

"I can't argue with you on that," he admitted. Chanel smirked. Jeff left the room and returned with his cell phone.

"What's up man? Where you at right now?" I need you to stop by and fix me up... Sure... I'll see you in a moment." With the deal in motion Jeff ended the call. He then looked at Chanel.

"He'll be here in half an hour."

While they sat around waiting for the dope-boy to come, Jasmine decided to have a few shots from the bar. Chanel caught Jeff staring at Jasmine multiple times. She knew what that look insinuated.

"It's not going to happen," Chanel informed him. He knew what Chanel was referring to.

"How can I make it work?" Jeff asked.

"Nothing in the world. She's not for sale," Chanel placed an emphasis on her response.

"That's too bad," Jeff said as he shook his head.

"Can I use your bathroom?" Jasmine asked.

"Sure. You want me to show you where it's at?" Jeff asked, catching a playful elbow from Chanel.

"She's fine. I'll show her," Chanel said.

"That she is," Jeff mumbled as Chanel and Jasmine headed to the bathroom. Once inside, Chanel looked at her watch.

"It's past a half hour. If this guy isn't here in the next ten minutes we're out of here," Chanel advised Jasmine who was using the toilet.

"If we can't score here, I know a guy," Jasmine commented.

"Well, we just may have to go to your guy. I think this might be a bust," Chanel responded.

As the two women were walking down the hallway, they heard what appeared to be a few men in the living room with Jeff. Chanel stopped dead in her tracks and told Jasmine to wait. They listened to the conversation.

"I thought you were out of town. I got your money and waited for your return," Jeff told the man without a name. Jasmine had her back against the wall as Chanel peeked around the corner to see what was going on. There were two men standing by the front door, and someone was sitting on the couch. Apparently, he was the main man.

"You have a nice place here, and I'm the reason you live in such comfort. Would that be an accurate statement?"

"Come on man, you know I have nothing but respect for you, and I would never cross you in any way," Jeff assured him.

The man on the couch clapped as if he was giving Jeff a standing ovation for a job well done. "The one thing that I take pride in is being a good judge of character, at least up to this point," the man explained as his henchmen took hold of Jeff and tied him to a chair.

"Come on man, I didn't do anything." Jeff tried to explain, but his pleas fell onto deaf ears.

"I not only know that you've been getting high on my product, I also know that you've been stealing money from me." The man smiled while his men pulled Jeff's shirt sleeve up. Jeff began to panic.

"I have something made especially for you," the man said as he pulled a syringe from his suit jacket.

"Don't do this man. I would work for free until I pay you back. Please don't do this," Jeff begged. As Jeff was held down, the syringe was given to the other man. Jeff gave it one last effort to fight them off, but one of the men punched him hard in the stomach, knocking the wind out of him. The other guy snatched the lamp from its stand and wrapped the cord around Jeff's arm while searching for a vein. The syringe was filled with pure heroin and a concoction that was powerful enough to kill an elephant.

The drug instantly took its toll as Jeff fell limp and turned pale. His body locked up and twitched violently. A foreign substance came out of his mouth and blood seeped from his eyes. In seconds, Jeff' was dead.

"Check his fucking pulse. Make sure he's dead," the boss ordered. After checking his pulse, the three of them left the house. Chanel and Jasmine cautiously crept their way into the living room and saw Jeff'. His eyes were open and lifeless.

"Is he dead?" Jasmine asked as she was afraid to move.

"Yeah, he's dead. Let's get out of here," Chanel replied.

Chanel and Jasmine rushed out of the house, hoping to escape from what they had witnessed — a forced drug overdose orchestrated by three men demanding revenge and respect. The boss was a major drug supplier who provided Jeff with the drugs he passed on to his clientele. Not only was Jeff a steady source of heroin, he was Chanel's friend. Watching him strapped to a chair, shirt sleeve raised, and a syringe embedded into his skin, was unimaginable. Although Chanel and Jasmine were coming down from a high, what took place was real. Jeff's open and lifeless eyes were tattooed into their brains; most likely, forever.

Rational thought often times becomes tainted by one's altered perception of reality. Chanel and Jasmine searched for clarity. *Should we have done something? Is it our fault?*

"They killed him," Jasmine yelled.

"You're bugging right now," Chanel spoke.

"Bugging? You really think that I'm bugging? A guy gets killed and we took off as if nothing happened," Jasmine vented.

Chanel stopped the car, waiting for the light to turn green. She knew that Jasmine was scared. "Listen," Chanel said. "We did nothing wrong, and there's nothing we could have done to save Jeff. He was already dead."

"I just wished we could have helped." Jasmine replied.

Chanel grabbed Jasmine's hand and looked into her eyes. "We did nothing wrong. We're going to meet another dealer and get fucked up and put this shit behind us." Chanel leaned forward and kissed Jasmine's lips. Chanel's eyes fixated on the colors in the sky; an eerie shade of red and orange swallowed the day's final glimpse of light. The traffic light turned green. People began honking their horns, prompting Chanel to drive forward.

* * *

Drugs addicts, like Chanel and Jasmine, reject their reality and use drugs to create an altered mental state meant to calm their soul and release their demons. Each change in the human brain shapes their reality.

The two of them found another dealer and wasted no time getting back to their room. The image of Jeff's open and lifeless eyes needed to be erased; at least for the moment. To do so, required a heavy dose of heroin. As the mood-altering effects of the heroin took hold, the image of Jeff's open and lifeless eyes slid into darkness.

"I see you," Jasmine said to Chanel as she spoke with closed eyes.

"As I see you," Chanel replied and then kissed Jasmine on her lips. The two of them began their flight through a universe constructed of tranquility and a demon-free environment.

Why would anyone give this up? Chanel thought. Why would any sane individual, coherent or not, trade the liberated path to freedom for abstinence? Life's a relentless bitch with no compassionate karma to be had. Peace is but the smallest window in a world of large, black holes. Climbing through one is quite the task.

"I can feel the blood running through my body," Jasmine said.

Chanel began to chuckle at Jasmine's humor. "I think that's how it's supposed to work unless you're dead." Chanel loved this side of her friend; the humor and vibrancy were exciting. Chanel couldn't do anything but laugh. They enjoyed their high and the escape to another world. Minutes later they were asleep; forgetting, for the moment, Jeff's open and lifeless eyes.

*   *   *

Chanel dove into the swimming pool. It had been some time since she had taken a swim, and today seemed like the perfect time to do so. As Chanel came up for air, she saw other swimmers jumping into the water. One swimmer drew her attention. It was Dr. Smith, her psychologist. Chanel swam across the pool to greet her.

"You don't look half bad in a swimming suit."

Smith turned around and saw Chanel. "What are you doing here?" Smith asked in a concerned tone, not expecting to be seen in a swimming pool with one of her clients.

"You suggested I swim, so here I am."

"Yes, but not on Sundays when I swim at this pool. I cannot be seen with you outside of my office."

"Lighten up. Besides, I was here first," Chanel said as she back paddled.

As Smith swam towards the other side of the pool, Chanel joined her. Smith became more uncomfortable.

"Can you at least stop following me," Smith demanded.

"I have a question. Let me ask it and I'll leave. I promise." Smith was apprehensive but felt as if she had no choice but to let her ask the question.

"One question and then you must leave," Smith shot back.

"Did I meet your expectations?"

"What, what do you mean?" Smith asked.

"Come on counselor, you know what I mean." Chanel swam over and grabbed hold of the rail. Smith followed her, expecting Chanel to explain her question. "You have an aura about you, one that attracts people. I like talking to you because it helps me."

"Well, I'm glad you're able to open up to me, but let's go back to your question. What expectations are you talking about?" Smith replied.

"Curiosity always does it. Now I have something that you want. You see, I can play this game too," Chanel explained.

"What game? I'm not playing any game."

"But you are. You just don't know it yet," Chanel replied.

Chanel moved closer, making Smith feel more uncomfortable. Chanel then moved close enough to whisper into Smith's ear. By this time, their breasts touched, causing Smith to believe that she had lost control.

"I can feel your heart beating faster and your breathing is becoming irregular. Do I make you uncomfortable?"

"No!" Smith shot back.

Chanel knew that she had stripped Smith of whatever power she thought she had. Now Smith was at the mercy of Chanel's wrath. "I think you're in over your head," Chanel said. By now the pool was empty; just the two of them. Chanel ran her hand over the side of Smith's face then cradled her waist.

"What are you doing?" Smith was unable to move. Chanel kissed her neck. She remained frozen, hoping that Chanel would go away. Chanel felt Smith's nipples and moved her hand into Smith's bottoms.

Although they were in a pool, Chanel felt the moisture on the tips of her fingers. Smith was so caught up in the moment that she didn't realize that her legs were wrapped around Chanel's waist. Chanel removed her hand and tasted the nectar.

"I guess we're more alike than you thought. And the expectations that I was talking about are your dreams. I know you've been dreaming about me." Chanel got out of the pool and left before Smith could speak a single word.

CHAPTER EIGHT

Victoria

Victoria stared through the bedroom window. Rain continued to fall, thunder pounded the house, and lighting illuminated the sky. Victoria placed her small hand on the window and felt the vibration.

"I'm sorry you're sad," she mumbled, hoping that her words would console Mother Nature's pain. Victoria wondered why the sky was so sad. She grabbed her stuffed-rabbit from its cage and went to find her mother. Lana was on the sofa drinking wine and watching television. She looked up and saw her daughter carrying Mr. Chuckles, the rabbit.

"Did the storm wake you and Mr. Chuckles?"

"Yes," Victoria answered and joined her mother on the sofa.

"I went to the window and saw the sky crying. I hope it stops. The sun won't come out if the sky is sad." Lana knew that the world was a cold place and had no discrimination as to who it chose to pulverize. Lana vowed to guard Victoria's life with her own and see to it that she was happy. But someday she would have to let go, allowing Victoria to become her own woman.

"I think you're a beautiful and courageous girl," Lana said.

Victoria opened her eyes, realizing that she had been dreaming. She sat up in the bed and brushed the strands of hair from her face. The dreams were vivid and real, suggesting that her mother was reaching out from the other side.

* * *

Victoria was flying to California, ready and anxious to begin a life-changing experience. As the plane approached the landing strip, Victoria saw the top of a dolphin racing across the ocean's surface. She was reminded of "*The Black River.*" As a young girl, Victoria's belief in the metaphysical allowed her mind to delve into the supernatural.

> *I wouldn't say my mother was deceptive nor vindictive, at least not towards me, Victoria thought. If Lana used made-up stories because of my youthfulness, then I accept her efforts to accommodate me. I think my mother believed in the theurgical river, better known as" The Black River." But Lana was good at hiding her secrets. Over time, Victoria had lost faith in the presence of the mysterious river, questioning how such a place could exist.*

* * *

While Victoria enjoyed the fact that Valerie was genuine and sincere, she was aware of her awkwardness. Victoria believed that one's past was filled with skeletons; some buried and others seen by the naked eye. Perhaps that applied to Valerie.

"Is there anything that I can do?" Valerie asked as she entered Victoria's suite.

Victoria sat on the sofa with her legs crossed. "I'm fine for now," she answered. "You seem a bit tense for someone who claims to be assertive." Victoria could be an intimidating woman, making it difficult for Valerie to relax.

"I don't think being assertive is fitting for the job," Valerie said.

"Why not?" Victoria asked. "I'd rather you be yourself, and not the watered-down version." She closed her eyes, stretched her legs, and fell asleep on the sofa. Valerie left to unpack their luggage.

The sound of water moved in with a destructive force. Victoria's eyes were dull and filled with a mysterious intent. The water began to fill her lungs, causing her mind to drift into a self-analyses. We often experience moments of invariable acts of certitude, a lack of judgement when we understand nothing. Perhaps we grasp strains of knowledge for deceitful purposes to be used against an adversary.

Victoria's lungs were burning from a lack of air. Panic set in as she struggled to reach the surface. Despite her efforts, she sank even deeper. Death's hand had a powerful grip on Victoria's soul, allowing her to imagine the freedom she was about to experience. With a smile on her face, Victoria submitted to the undercurrents, hoping to encounter the ultimate ecstasy.

Victoria coughed up fluid as if her lungs were filled with water. Her body struggled to awaken from her dream. While unpleasant, it was one of many dreams where she envisioned herself drowning in the river. An individual stood on the other side of the water and watched Victoria submit to death.

Victoria left the sofa and drank a glass of cold water. She then found Valerie sleeping in the bedroom. Victoria approached the bed and imagined Valerie to be the sleeping beauty. It was perplexing how complete strangers held power over our conscious thoughts, making us feel obligated to protect them and be emotionally available, Victoria thought.

Victoria sat on the side of the bed, brushed the hair from Valerie's face; fully mesmerized by her beauty. Victoria had no idea why she climbed into Valerie's bed. Perhaps it reminded her of the nights she shared with her mother.

Victoria woke when Valerie suddenly sat up in the bed. Valerie then realized that Victoria was under the covers with her. Unable to speak, Valerie tried to process the fact that Victoria was on top of her. Victoria smiled and rolled off.

"It's not like we had sex. Relax." Victoria then closed her eyes and went back to sleep.

* * *

Victoria and Valerie sat in the backseat as the driver drove them to look at some homes in the more prestigious areas of Los Angeles, California. Victoria looked out the window as the people moved about in their perceived agendas. While some appeared to be happy, they were most likely disturbed on the inside. Victoria saw life as it was shown to her; not the ugliness, anger, and rage that sometimes emerges when it's too late.

The car stopped in a small community next to a private lake. Victoria stepped from the car and was immediately drawn to the large body of water.

"Who owns the lake?" Victoria asked the moment the realtor approached them.

"The Stevenson's," replied the realtor.

Victoria's gaze never left the water. She was caught up in its aura, mesmerized by its unintentional enchantment. "I want it," Victoria demanded.

"It's not for sale," the realtor said as Victoria turned to face her.

"Everything is for sale," Victoria added. She then asked Valerie to hand her a checkbook.

"Give yourself a bonus and make this happen." While Victoria wasn't arrogant nor full of herself, she was persistent when she wanted something.

"I'll see what I can do," the realtor replied.

CHAPTER NINE

Chanel

Chanel and Jasmine joked around as they chauffeured each other in a shopping cart at the grocery store, acting like children in an amusement park. Jasmine sat in the cart eating dry cereal while encouraging Chanel to push faster. Other shoppers considered Chanel and Jasmine to be a bit crazy or high on drugs. As Chanel turned the corner, the shopping cart ran out-of-control causing Jasmine to roll out of the cart and onto the floor.

A very large security man quickly approached them, demanding that they leave the store. Jasmine rose to her feet and approached the security guard; so close that she could feel his heartbeat. He was taken by Jasmine's sexual attraction.

"I have to ask you to leave, but if you can quiet down a bit, I can let you stay." The man spoke with a nervous tone to his voice.

"We can do that," Chanel added as Jasmine reached for his belt buckle and began to pull his pants down. He was wearing a pair of briefs a size too small and discolored from years of wear. The girls broke into laughter and began running away.

"Fuck you, fat ass?" Jasmine yelled, lifting her dress and smacking her ass. The guard pulled his pants up and ran after them. But he was no match for the young women racing to their car. While Chanel drove off, Jasmine found some lively music on the radio and moved to the beat. Chanel looked at Jasmine out of the corner of her eye and smiled. Jasmine was full of life, careless and void of sound judgement. It was as if the two of them were entangled into the same web. They ended the venture by returning to their hotel room for the night.

*   *   *

Jasmine taught me so much about love and compassion. I loved everything about her. I still remember my first orgasm. Jasmine was sexually liberated and more in tune with her body. She wanted to free me from my past and to embrace my sexuality. I learned to please myself through her touch as she repealed the life sentence in my mental prison.

The first taste of Jasmine's lips was intoxicating. My heart pounded with curiosity and anticipation as to what was coming next. As Jasmine explored my neck with sensuous kisses, my breathing grew deeper and faster. Although I was unsure what was about to happen, I trusted Jasmine.

I was dressed in a t-shirt and a pair of panties. I wasn't wearing a bra and my nipples protruded through the fabric. She reached her hand under and touched my breasts, causing my body to react in ways not yet discovered. She took her other hand, inserting her fingers into me. At first, I tensed up, but seconds later I spread my legs and welcomed her advances. She showered my clitoris with wet kisses. Jasmine then mounted me and placed her tongue deep into my mouth. She looked into my eyes and told me that she loved me.

Jasmine removed her shirt and undid her bra and my shirt and panties as well. I slipped into a different world as Jasmine kissed my inner thighs. The moment Jasmine's tongue entered my vagina, I jumped from the bed. Jasmine laughed and told me to relax. I slid back onto the bed and let Jasmine part my vagina and kiss it multiple times. I arched my back and grabbed a hand full of Jasmine's hair. I had never felt this way before and wanted more. By now, Jasmine had moved her face flush to my vagina. I screamed with pleasure and felt totally consumed by her. My body produced a slow and deep climax as I squeezed out my final ounce of body fluid.

* * *

Chanel walked into Dr. Smith's office and sat in the familiar incliner near the window ledge. Smith tried her best to appear cordial and unnerved. Chanel knew that their previous encounter at the pool was likely engraved into Smith's brain. It was obvious that Chanel never regretted her past behavior.

"Do you believe that dreams are windows to reality?" Chanel asked.

"They can be," answered Smith. "Dreams often times originate from actual events you've experienced."

"Sometimes I feel as if I'm somewhere else. Perhaps the life I'm living is tied to another soul. I know it sounds crazy, but it's the truth," Chanel admitted.

"I think you're on a journey to find yourself, and during such a quest you'll feel a bit out of touch."

"You're quite the woman, aren't you?" Chanel asked. "I see you. Your eyes tell me things that your mouth would never utter." Chanel approached Smith, circling her like a lioness approaching her prey. Stirring the emotions of someone she's about to conquer, was the power that Chanel craved. As Smith was about to object to Chanel's antics, Chanel took her seat. Smith backed off.

"Are you attracted to women Dr. Smith?"

Smith cleared her throat before speaking. "I think that is an inappropriate question."

"Come on now. We're well past the ethical bullshit you're about to shoot my way. You're so full of shit." Chanel shot back.

"Perhaps I'm missing something here," Smith replied. "I'm the one whose been assigned to handle your care. So, I don't have to answer your questions." Chanel began to clap.

"And there you go again. I knew this side of you would come out." Chanel spoke with a touch of sarcasm. "The thing about me is the fact that I don't hide who I am. I know my stories about the sexual escapades leave your panties wet. But I'm not at all offended. It's quite flattering."

"You're wrong, and I will terminate your sessions if you think you can play games with me," Smith shot back. While unmoved, Chanel got up from her chair and approached Smith.

"That day in the pool. Your juices tasted like honey on the tips of my fingers, and your mourns stirred passion." As Chanel talked, she moved her hands along Dr. Smith's shoulders. Then she moved down to her breast, feeling her erect nipples growing harder by the second. Smith had no idea how this woman was able to make her feel helpless. She closed her eyes and drifted into another reality, hoping this would last for a lifetime. Those who are unpredictable stand to be the most dangerous, and there's no telling how far they're willing to go. Smith bolted from her chair and put some distance between herself and Chanel.

"This has to stop," Smith yelled. Those were the only words she managed to say. Chanel smiled and approached Smith again. She then backed Smith into a corner and kissed her lips.

"Just when we think we're in control, we find out the complete opposite. I'll see you next week Dr. Smith." With that, Chanel left Smith to her thoughts.

*   *   *

"Shit!" Chanel said. She was looking everywhere for the silver dolphin her mother had given to her when she was a little girl. It was the only reminder she had of her mother and she couldn't find it. Chanel just noticed that it was missing and was about to panic. She didn't even remember the last time that she had worn the silver dolphin.

The majority of the world is ravaged with distant memories, a past that never rests. While it appeared as though Chanel held it all together, she was about to break. She climbed into her bed and was overcome by a rush of emotions. For someone who appeared to be in control, this was unusual. The barriers were cracked, allowing Chanel to release her misery through buckets of tears. If only for a moment, the release of emotions helped cleanse her soul.

Being strong is a task within itself, and even then, strength always has its breaking point. Pain is a complicated emotion, leaving someone to question the location of its source. If undiscovered, the pain persists like an open wound; never allowing the individual to live in a contented state. While the world continues to grow, there are billions of lifeless-people left to occupy space; a lonely place for you and your history to survive. Chanel turned to the only place that brought her peace — the next high.

CHAPTER TEN

Victoria

Victoria walked to the lake and allowed the cold water to run between her toes. The sun rays bounced off the water's surface, complementing the bluest sky Victoria had ever seen. Valerie walked onto the dock and joined Victoria near the water's edge. The owners had agreed to sell the lake, but not their home. And that was okay with Victoria.

"Can I do anything?" Valerie asked.

"Not at the moment," Victoria said as she gazed into the open water.

"You must really enjoy swimming to have purchased the lake at such an expensive price."

"I can't swim," Victoria replied. Valerie was confused.

"Then why did you buy it?" Valerie asked.

"When I was a little girl, my mother told me stories about *"The Black River,"* and how magical it was. She believed that the river was some gateway to happiness and true love. My mother was a dreamer, a woman with quite an imagination. I was young and had no reason to doubt such a place." As Victoria shared stories of her past, Valerie saw the sadness in her eyes, and the courage that allowed her to share her feelings.

"I think a place like that could actually exist," Valerie added.

"Maybe in another lifetime," Victoria replied.

"What happened to your mother, if you don't mind me asking?"

"She died of a heart attack." Valerie believed that there was more to this story.

Although Victoria was young, loneliness had aged her soul.

"Some things are difficult to believe, but that's the complexity of life. We can't explain everything, and that's okay. We can choose to believe in the implausible and allow it to shape our purpose for the better good," Valerie explained.

"You're quite the woman aren't you Ms. Valerie?" Victoria turned and headed for the gate.

> *I wonder if you can see me. Can you look past the glitz and glamour and see the ugliness hidden by my designer-labeled clothes? Perception paints illusions that are hidden to the naked eye; showing the world what I allow it to see. Internal scars are most likely to remain buried for years; perhaps forever. I can only hide behind the wealth until it wears off like yesterday's makeup.*

* * *

Victoria found Valerie in the kitchen and took a seat at the table. Normally, Victoria would already be up and well into her day. Valerie noticed a necklace around Victoria's neck that she'd never seen before.

"You never told me that you like dolphins." Victoria looked around as if she was talking to someone else.

"How did you come up with that?" Victoria seemed to be a bit confused.

"Your neck, the dolphin pendant," Valerie replied as she pointed to the necklace. Victoria grabbed it followed by a brief moment of silence.

"It's not mine. It belongs to someone I'm trying to locate so I can return it." Victoria thought back to the day that she and Chanel met at the masquerade event. Chanel held a mysterious energy that drew Victoria's attention. Her large, dark eyes held a sense of familiarity as if the two of them had met before.

Victoria had reached out to Gerald Day, the elder billionaire who had a hard-on for young girls. Unfortunately, it was a dead end. Day was out of the country and was unable to be reached.

"How about you show me around, you know, be my guide?" Victoria asked Valerie. "If I'm going to embrace my new journey, I need to fully commit to being open." Change wasn't something that Victoria was accustomed to and being optimistic about her new life carried a certain degree of risk.

"I'm not really a club kind of gal, and to be honest, I have no idea as to where we should go," Valerie admitted. Victoria wasn't surprised that Valerie was dull and unadventurous. Perhaps bringing Valerie along was a mistake. Maybe this was a journey that Victoria should travel on her won. There were so many questions that needed to be asked, and even more that needed to be answered. Sometimes you need to lose yourself in order to discover who you are.

Victoria wore a black dress that hugged her petite frame like a second layer of skin. Her hair hung well below her shoulders and she smelled of a vanilla fragrance with a touch of honey. Her dark eyes were stunning; the full-lips complimented her youthful facial features; and the Alexander McQueen pumps matched the fire-red handbag that she clutched. Valerie walked into the room and was stunned.

"You're beautiful."

"Aren't we all," Victoria replied.

"You know, I don't mind tagging along with you. After all you are my boss."

"It's fine, besides, I tend to mingle better on my own." Victoria had decided to attend a club called BED, and she actually knew the owner of the establishment. Steven, the club owner, had ties to a foundation out of Toronto, Canada. Steven, a billionaire philanthropist, had been Lana's friend. He sent a car to pick up Victoria, promising her nothing short of a good time.

CHAPTER ELEVEN

Chanel

I felt him deep inside of me. My need to reach the ultimate orgasm was strong. But this wasn't about him, this was about me. People have the misconception that women can't be sexually liberated and in control of their desires. His eyes told me that I was a goddess, a woman who fulfilled his needs. He gripped my waist tighter as I rode his shaft slowly, encouraging him to master my every move.

His erection provided a bit of pain with a mountain of pleasure. I slid up and down his rod, biting my lip as my movements increased. Moans filled the air while my fingernails dug into his chest; inching closer to a massive climax. I rubbed myself with one hand while pinching my nipple with the other; rolling on my side and guiding his juice-covered penis back into my swollen wound. His strokes were long and sensual and quicker as he picked up the pace. I wanted to be dominated if only for a brief moment. His name or who he was didn't matter. He was merely a stepping- stone to a different kind of high; one that made me feel needed like never before.

* * *

Chanel hated the idea of working a mundane 9 to 5 job. She was employed as a bottle girl at the night club that welcomed her charm. The club was an elite business that catered to the rich and famous, while welcoming the working class and the LGBT community. Each group had their special location within the club.

Chanel wore a pair of fishnet stockings, cut-off shorts, and a revealing low-cut tank top. Being hounded by men who ogled her body, fit well into Chanel's wheelhouse. Men weren't the cleverest when it involved a beautiful woman. Women held a power that few men could fully comprehend. People danced to the music and mingled amongst the crowd as if the night would soon come to an end. Although Chanel was on the clock, this was the environment where she excelled. While moving across the floor, someone grabbed her hand. It was a male actor who Chanel knew.

"Would you mind joining us?" he asked.

"I wish I could, but it's against club policy. Sorry."

"There's no fun in that. I tell you what. A friend of mine is having an after party. You should come." While the actor was persistent, his eyes held Chanel's attention.

"I'll see what I can do," Chanel replied.

"You do that," the actor added as he gave Chanel his number.

While Chanel's mind was stuck on the actor, she delivered more bottles to the customers. As she carried a tray of bottles, someone bumped into her and knocked the tray to the floor. Chanel began cleaning up the mess when a beautiful woman dressed in a black dress came strutting by.

CHAPTER TWELVE

Victoria

Steven saw to it that Victoria was escorted to the club. The club was lavish and considered to be one of the elite nightspots in the area. She even had her own sky box. There were three levels and a VIP section furnished with canopy beds and leather sofas. While Victoria wasn't a party type of woman, she had decided to throw herself into the new journey.

Steven was out of town on business and unable to show her around the club. Instead, he advised his staff to embrace her, and that she shouldn't pay for anything. As Victoria was escorted to a VIP section, she came upon an employee who was cleaning spilled drinks and broken glass from the floor. Victoria carefully walked around the accident and headed to the elevator. As the doors closed, Victoria made eye contact with the employee. While their eyes connected briefly, it felt as if it was a lifetime. There was a lingering familiarity that sharpened Victoria's curiosity.

Her sky box was connected to another VIP section whose occupants wasted no time in introducing themselves. The most privileged people of society can be a bit repulsive as they try to one-up the others; complete with exaggerated accolades and their financial standing. Victoria found herself drowning in boredom, hoping that someone would rescue her.

She left her seat and walked to the large glass window. The lower level was filled with the working class people; those who worked long hours in corporate America, hoping to climb the ladder of success.

Victoria saw nothing but happiness as the people danced, drank, and had a good time. Tonight was their way of escaping the stress-filled life of the working person. Victoria excused herself and headed to the lower level. Once she found her way to the dance floor, she felt the pulsating music as it pumped throughout her body. It was vibrant and electric as if she was in the epic center of a rave. There wasn't a single soul bragging about how much money they made, their accomplishments nor anything work related. There were bottles passed around and glow sticks used to light up the dance floor. Victoria was drinking champagne and dancing like tonight was her last night.

A beautiful Asian girl approached Victoria and began to dance with her. Victoria was feeling the effects of the alcohol as her body responded to the music. The girl moved close and began to touch Victoria's body. While she felt this to be a bit intimidating, it was arousing as well. What Victoria didn't know was the fact that each floor catered to a different group of people. She was not aware that the lower level was for the lesbian community.

"Have you ever tried a *Molly*?" The girl yelled over the loud music. Victoria had no idea what she was talking about, and the ignorance was written all over her face.

"Don't worry. Just try it. I promise you'll be fine." The girl told Victoria to stick her tongue out. The girl opened the capsule and poured the powdery substance on her tongue, telling Victoria to down it with a drink. It tasted bitter, like swallowing crushed Advil. The girl swallowed a *Molly* as well. The two of them continued to dance. Some thirty-minutes later, Victoria felt alive, unlike anything she had ever experienced before. She was floating on an imaginary cloud without a worry in the world.

"How do you feel?" The girl asked.

"Like I'm on a fucking roller coaster. I feel great!"

"Follow me," the girl said as she grabbed hold of Victoria's hand and led her to the girl's room. Once inside, they entered a stall. Victoria assumed it was where they could take another *Molly,* but that was not the case.

Victoria was now able to see what the girl looked like and she was beautiful, like one of those Victoria Secret models. Victoria was higher than before and her body was on fire.

"What is your name?" Victoria asked.

"Cheri," she replied while pushing Victoria against the wall and began kissing her passionately. This was definitely unchartered territory for Victoria and to be honest, she had submerged herself into the moment with no regrets. Cheri pulled Victoria's panties down and lifted her dress. She kissed Victoria's thighs and squeezed the back of her legs. Victoria's heart rate increased as she asked for more. Cheri felt the heat from Victoria's vagina as she inched closer to the sacred place.

Cheri parted Victoria's vaginal lips with her fingers and tasted her. Victoria nearly clasped her legs together as the sensation from Cheri's tongue sent shock waves throughout her body. There was a moment, one that couldn't be defined nor explained with any level of clarity; just one that felt right and purposeful. This was one of those moments. Victoria looked down at Cheri who returned her gaze and ate from her womb like the last meal she'd be able to devour. Light moans followed as she grabbed a hand full of Cheri's hair and fed her snatch to the hungry deviant. There had never been a time that Victoria had ever thought that she would find herself in this position; adventurous and open to change.

Cheri's face was covered with juices, and it only made her more eager to please. She told Victoria to turn around and bend over. Cheri came from behind and began kissing her neck as she put her fingers inside the soaking vagina. Victoria arched her back while the pleasure bombarded her like an array of emotions. Her moans grew louder as Cheri fingered her at a faster pace. Victoria came so hard that there was nectar running down her legs.

The two of them took a few moments to regain their composure before returning to the dance floor. In time, the club was about to close. For Cheri, this evening was not a situation for her. But for Victoria, this unforgettable evening was just the beginning of her new journey.

Victoria's driver pulled up at a red light as she looked out the window. The *Molly* had worn off and brought Victoria back down from cloud nine. She was tired and in need of some sleep. Something drew Victoria's attention. It was a girl on the side of the road.

CHAPTER THIRTEEN

Chanel

TWENTY-MINUTES EARLIER:

Chanel had called Jasmine numerous times, but she didn't answer. There was no telling what she had going on. Chanel had received a lot of tips working tables and it was time to call it a night. While Jasmine always called to make sure Chanel made it home after work, there was no call tonight. Jasmine was a wild card, always on the go. There wasn't another person in the world that Chanel trusted.

Chanel sat on the edge of her bed dealing with her thoughts. Being alone was agonizing. Isolation was what Chanel feared the most, and there wasn't a remedy for what she deemed to be incurable. Although it was late, she did the one thing that maintained her balance; call someone to vent.

"Do you have any idea what time it is?" Dr. Smith asked the moment she answered the phone. She knew it was Chanel from the number on the phone.

"You said to call whenever I wanted to talk."

"Yeah, reasonable hours. Give me a second," Smith said as she slid out of bed hoping not to wake her husband.

"Hello, you still there?" Chanel asked.

"Yeah, I'm here," Smith replied. "What is it that you want to talk about?" A few silent seconds passed.

"Sometimes I wish I could disappear, and never come back. Hide the scars and what's hidden in my head."

"We all have problems in life and dealing with them is part of the healing process," Smith added. "But your choosing to run from your problems aren't healing nor providing an outlet for you to escape."

"And what do you suggest Dr. Smith?"

"I suggest that you face your problems and don't lose sight of the task at hand."

"Do I make you nervous?" Chanel's question caught Smith off guard.

"Not at all, but I do feel as if I've allowed you to compromise my position, and I'll never allow that to happen again."

"You sure about that?" Chanel asked as she moved to her couch to lie down. She stretched out and closed her eyes.

"I'm not playing your games anymore, and I will not tolerate your insolence," Smith snapped. Chanel released a slight laughter.

"Look at you, standing up for yourself. I think the two of us work great together. You have this ability to open me up, making me feel free and capable. I wish I had that power over myself. Maybe that's why I choose to be sexually liberated and use drugs as a way of maintaining my sanity." Chanel explained.

"You're suffering Ms. Rosenthal, and if you don't find a solution to what's causing your discontent, it will only get worse."

"Do you think that I'm broken?" Chanel asked.

"Broken is a strong word. I think that you are more challenged than anything."

"Hmmmm... That's all you came up with?" Chanel knew the answers to her questions, and what made her tick. Dr. Smith was only a means to an end. Nothing really mattered to Chanel, and life was a constant rotation of mystery. You never know what each day would present. Maybe that's what makes life interesting.

"I want to help you, but first you have to trust the process, and allow it to work for you. You're here for a reason. You're sick and you need to acknowledge that," Smith explained.

"I have a love for words, writing how I feel on the inside," Chanel said. "Poetry helps me to be myself during times when I question what I want out of life. It's like I'm dancing along the shadows of death. Would you like to hear one of my poems?"

"Sure, why not."

More than likely.

Despite the pain that consumes me,
carries me on dark clouds and thunderstorms.
Lighting strikes me.

More than likely.

I'm dead and gone.
Perhaps forgotten,

More than likely.

When Chanel finished, Smith was at a loss for words. It was both beautiful and dark.

"You didn't like it?" questioned Chanel.

"I strongly enjoyed it. I just have to let it settle in."

"Some pain digs deeper than others, and it's hard to figure it out. I think I have one of those pains. One I'll never be able to get rid of," Chanel explained.

"You give it too much power over your life. I don't want you to give in to your circumstances. Fight against it rather than forfeit your will power moving forward," Smith replied. They talked a bit longer before Smith had to call it a night.

*   *   *

Chanel walked into the bathroom and looked at herself in the mirror. While she still looked exceptional on the outside, her insides suffered an ongoing nightmare. Chanel let her hair down and forced a smile that faded quickly. Her mood shifted as well. She reached for the razor on the edge of the tub, removing the blade from its casing. Chanel put the blade against her wrist and took a deep breath. Her heart was pounding. This was the answer to it all and was something that she had been wanting to do. People often times find something to live for in the moment that dying became an option. But for Chanel, even with a blade pressed against her wrist, she still felt the same.

She wanted to die as she ran the blade across her wrist and felt her skin open. She dropped the blade. Chanel sat with her back against the tub and watched her wrist leak blood from her body.

Chanel snapped out of her thoughts, questioning whether they were real. She looked into the mirror, wondering if this was how it would have felt. But a boring death was contrary to who she was. When she dies, it must be an exciting departure. Chanel grabbed the blade and began cutting her hair. She needed to feel different, and this was the beginning.

CHAPTER FOURTEEN

Victoria

There was never a time in Victoria's young life when she felt drawn to people. Some might say she was on the quiet side. But Victoria's persona was about to change. The transformation began when she found an unconscious young lady lying on the side of the road.

It was obvious that the lady needed medical attention. The driver and Victoria rushed her to a nearby hospital. In an earlier time, Victoria might have left the girl at the hospital and moved on. But for some reason, she chose to wait and see if the lady recovered.

The doctor entered the waiting room. "Ma'am, are you related to the young lady?" He then looked at the medical chart. "Jasmine Winters is her name."

"No," Victoria said. "I found her on the side of the road. Is she alright?"

"She's fine, thanks to you. You can see her now." The doctor turned and walked away.

Victoria walked down the hallway and entered the hospital room. "I guess you're the one I have to thank for saving my life," Jasmine said as she sat up in her bed and brushed the hair from her face.

"I figured you were in trouble, and I did what any decent human being would have done."

"Thank you. You saved my life for sure." It was obvious to Jasmine that Victoria came from a different world; not a poverty-stricken place filled with skeletons of the past. Victoria's dress and expensive-looking high heels spelled privilege. Even the way she sat with her hands in her lap while maintaining a good posture were hints of a different social class.

"Can I get you anything. Food, something to drink?" Victoria offered.

"I'm fine. You're not from around here, are you?" Jasmine asked.

"Is it that obvious?" Victoria responded with a smile on her face.

"Yes. You're so formal and well spoken. You stand out for sure."

"I'm from Canada, but I live here now. I just moved to the states for a fresh start." Victoria explained.

"I'm Jasmine. The least I can do is offer a proper introduction. I hate that we had to meet under such circumstances."

"I'm Victoria, and the circumstances are fine."

Jasmine got out of the bed and retrieved her clothes from the closet. "A drug overdose," Jasmine said as she pulled her jeans up. Victoria was a bit surprised by Jasmine's routine announcement of having overdosed on drugs.

"I had a drug overdose. I know you're wondering what happened on the side of the road. That's it. I took too much and overdosed."

"I took a *Molly* a few hours ago," Victoria said. Jasmine nearly fell to the floor with laughter. It was obvious that Victoria was as green as they come, and Jasmine found her to be hilarious.

"I can take you to your car if you like," Victoria asked.

"Sure!" Jasmine replied. The two of them bailed before the doctor came back.

"I owe you a night on the town, and I will not accept no for an answer," Jasmine announced.

"What do you have in mind?" Victoria asked.

"I never plan ahead. I'm more of a just do it kind of gal. Impromptu, so to speak," Jasmine explained.

Victoria instructed the driver where to go and turned to face Jasmine. "I have no idea what you have going on, but I have a proposition if you're interested."

Jasmine looked at her with a puzzled expression. "I'm listening."

"Since I have no idea what I'm doing here in the states, I have no direction. If you show me around, I'll pay you for your time."

"Why would you have to pay me for that?" Jasmine asked.

"I don't mind paying you for your time."

"You just saved my life." Jasmine opened the door as the driver pulled over. She got out of the car and turned towards Victoria. "Here's my number. Text me your address and we'll go from there." With that, Jasmine left Victoria and walked to her car.

* * *

Victoria climbed into the tub and watched the hot water cover her body like a second layer of skin. She relaxed and closed her eyes. The water gave birth to a distant memory of her mother.

> *Glass and other objects crashed to the floor. Lana yelled at Todd, one of her frequent lovers. I was young and oblivious to my mother's desperate cries to be loved. Since no relationship ever lasted more than a year, I was never emotionally connected to the men in her life nor did I question Lana's failed relationships during my childhood.*
>
> *Once the mayhem ended and Todd had left for the night, I found my mother in the wine cellar. I sat on the steps, waiting for Lana to emerge. She nearly dropped her bottle of wine when she saw me.*
>
> *"You scared me. What are you doing up ladybug?"*
>
> *"I heard the yelling and couldn't go back to sleep."*
>
> *"I'm sorry honey. Let's get you back to bed," Lana said. She grabbed my hand and escorted me back to the bedroom. Our bond was one that could only be shared by a mother and her daughter. We climbed into the bed and snuggled underneath the covers.*
>
> *"Can you tell me a story?" I asked.*
>
> *"A story. What do you want to hear my darling?"*
>
> *"The Black River!" I said.*
>
> *"The Black River isn't a real story, but I can make it into one," Lana explained as her finger touched Victoria's nose. Although I had never been to The Black River, I believed such*

a place existed. If the world was full of sadness and misfortune, there must be a magical place in a chaotic world?

I wanted to believe in the stories of The Black River, but they were more for Lana's comfort. Watching Lana deal with relationship issues deterred me from accepting the magical powers of the river. But the stories were compelling and spell binding. While Lana never shared all of the details that surrounded the river, she often times described how the sun's rays reflected off the water's surface.

It's easy to lose sight of what's in front of us, especially when we're trying to focus on everything around us. I think dying is much easier than living; dealing with the constant pressure pounding away at the exterior of our foundation. We all lose pieces of ourselves and spend most of our time trying to recover.

Victoria got out of the tub and wrapped herself in a dry towel. Recollections of her past were exhausting and painful. She felt like Lana had prevented her from flourishing into the next stage of her development. While there was a huge void in her life, she was determined that her new journey would be comprehensive. The United States was a melting pot filled with opportunities, and for her, it was just what she needed.

CHAPTER FIFTEEN

Chanel

While Chanel was sleeping, Jasmine entered the bedroom and dove on top of her. They had not seen each other in two days and were thrilled to be reunited.

"I've been calling you. I was worried." Chanel admitted.

"My phone died and there wasn't another one available. I was in the boondocks." Jasmine didn't want to tell Chanel that she had overdosed. Jasmine hated lying to her, but it was best to avoid a lengthy conversation. Although she'd seen Chanel overdose on multiple occasions, seeing Jasmine overdose would be serious. After all, Chanel couldn't die. She had tried too many times. But for Jasmine, it was most definitely plausible.

"So, what's the plan for today?" Jasmine asked. She didn't want to tell Chanel that she had met someone because the fact that she overdosed would be revealed.

"I don't know. I think I'll just use today to catch up on some sleep. Besides, Johnathan wants to see me," Chanel admitted.

"We should take a trip somewhere. You know, get away from everything," Jasmine suggested. The two of them always took time out to go somewhere and just unravel. While they were talking Chanel's nose began bleeding.

"Your nose," Jasmine pointed out. As of lately this had occurred more often. Chanel knew her medical condition wasn't ideal, but she felt a simple nosebleed couldn't be serious. She got up from her bed and headed to the shower. As the warm water tickled her skin, she buried her medical concerns. Jasmine entered the bathroom and proceeded to brush her teeth.

"Remember that rich girl I told you about when I attended that masquerade party in Canada?" Chanel asked.

"Vaguely. Why?" Jasmine questioned.

"I think I saw her the night I worked club BED."

"We all have a twin in the world. What are the odds of that actually happening?" Jasmine remarked.

"We didn't have the opportunity to see each other. It was just a brief gaze we shared," Chanel explained.

"It could have been anybody," Jasmine replied.

"Yeah. It could've." Chanel admitted. But there was no doubt in her mind that the girl was Victoria. She had the distinctive eyes and familiar gaze. It wasn't as if the two of them were friends or had significant ties to each other. Their encounter was brief.

* * *

Johnathan was a successful real estate broker, owner of an art gallery, and one of Chanel's clients. When Chanel began accumulating clients, she was not fond of being a sexual tool to satisfy a man's desires. But her sexual and drug-filled encounters served as a distraction to past trauma. Johnathan was more considerate than most of the male clients. He took care of her first and treated her with respect. They ate at five star establishments and attended lavish events. The two of them had just finished watching a live band performance.

"Did you enjoy yourself?" he asked.

"Of course. I thought it was nice."

"I'm having a party in the Hamptons in a few weeks. I think you should bring a plus one," Johnathan suggested.

"Let me see what I have planned for next week. I'll get back to you on that." While Chanel knew that her schedule was open next week, being unavailable was part of the act. She had mastered the art of seduction and taught herself to be without emotion. Men were attracted to being challenged; the thought of conquering a task was invigorating.

The world was connected by a similar need for pleasure; to feel, to want, and to be accepted. Each individual was presented with an undefined time interval; a space we occupied until death beckoned our presence.

She felt every inch of Johnathan's erection that filled her womb. Chanel consumed the pleasure, allowing her juices to flow without restraints. His lips were soft; his tongue tasted the sweet and bitterness in unison; and the intricate moments of pain and pleasure intensified the experience. He held on to Chanel's waist as she rode him like a raging bull.

Chanel stared into his eyes and took note of his imperfections and vulnerabilities. Like so many others, she invaded his mind and robbed him of his strength and control.

"Right there," Chanel moaned as she eagerly bounced on his erection. Johnathan's toes were curled as he couldn't hold back anymore. He came so hard it looked like he was having a seizure. Chanel closed her eyes and bit down on her lip, hoping to break the skin and taste her blood.

"I'm about to come, I'm coming!" she raged and grinded on him like a mad woman. Chanel reached her climax and collapsed. The two of them shared the moment. She pulled the covers over her naked body and closed her eyes. Johnathan reached over and held her hand. Chanel wasn't into cuddling with her clients. It was too personal. She opened her eyes and turned to face him as she pulled her hand away.

"You know my rules."

"I do, but I'm hoping we can change that. I haven't been able to get you out of my head," he admitted.

"Johnathan, you're married. This understanding between us is not a thing."

"I'm leaving my wife!" he blurted out. Chanel quickly sat up. "I want us to be together," Johnathan added.

Chanel wasn't looking to be in a relationship. The reason she had rules in place was so no one would activate her feelings. "Johnathan, you're a great man, but I'm not looking for a relationship. You should make things work with your wife."

"I'm in love with you. I don't want anyone else."

"I'm not fit to be with anyone. I'm sorry, I'm just not." Chanel got out of the bed and proceeded to get dressed. Johnathan had a look of defeat plastered on his face, and Chanel felt bad for him. Having said that, she grabbed her things and left without regrets.

CHAPTER SIXTEEN

Victoria

Jasmine pulled up to a massive estate located in one of the most prestigious neighborhoods in Los Angeles, California. The mansion was surrounded by a tall fence and iron gates meant to ban unwanted guests. Two stone lions stood guard next to the water fountain just south of the two large oak doors. For Jasmine, this was an unfamiliar sight for someone who lived on the other side of the tracks; not to mention the fact that it was owned by a woman no older than herself.

When Jasmine stepped from the car, Valerie stood near the driveway and greeted her.

"Hi, I'm Valerie. Victoria's assistant. She's waiting for you by the lake." Jasmine followed closely behind while looking over the beautiful landscape.

"The home is very nice. Does she own this place?" Jasmine asked while walking towards the lake.

"Yes, but there's another home being built, something more to her liking," Valerie replied. When they rounded the corner, the two of them got inside a golf cart. The house was breath taking and the grass was a bright-green color adorned with strategically planted flowers and shrubs.

The lake was inhabited by a flock of ducks and birds that seemed to float in the open sky. Victoria was on the other side of the lake with her feet dangling from the dock into the water. Victoria was so mesmerized by her thoughts that she never noticed Jasmine's arrival.

"Mind if I join you?" Jasmine asked while taking a seat next to Victoria. She then removed her shoes and submerged her feet into the water.

"Did you have trouble locating the place?" Victoria asked.

"Not at all. I know a guy that owns a home in Spring Hills. I'm kind of familiar with the area," Jasmine explained.

Victoria could tell that Jasmine was an energetic, high-spirited young lady; a welcome participant in Victoria's new journey.

"My best friend loves the water. You two definitely have that in common," Jasmine remarked.

"What makes you think that I like the water?" Victoria questioned.

"Valerie told me the reason you picked this place was because of the lake."

"I actually hate large bodies of water. There's something about it that makes me crazy," Victoria explained.

"Then why buy the lake? Who would actually purchase an entire lake?" Jasmine joked.

"I bought it because I'm intrigued by the things that drive my fears. It's like facing my biggest fear and learning to conquer it. Some things you can't master, and that's when we learn to co-exist," Victoria explained.

While Jasmine listened to Victoria's words, she found her to be a mystery and at the same time, quite alluring. Jasmine heard the fear in her voice and saw the courage in her eyes. She applauded Victoria's efforts to overcome her phobia.

"You're an interesting woman," Jasmine said.

"We all have distinctive qualities," Victoria explained. "It's what makes people seem complicated and filled with so many details. Besides, who wants simplicity, it's boring. What do you see when you look into the lake?"

Their eyes locked onto each other, followed by a moment of silence when Jasmine lost her train of thought. She saw something in Victoria's eyes, something that echoed so much familiarity that it scared her.

"It'll come to me," Jasmine said as she struggled with her thoughts.

Victoria looked into the endless sky and smiled at nothing in particular. "So, who is this friend of yours? Tell me what's she like?"

"Vibrant, full of life and personality. She gets me and I get her." As she talked, Victoria's mind drifted to Lana. She and her mother were close like that, and now that she thought about it, she had no one now. It was just her, and those who were employed by her. Victoria realized that she had no friends or family.

"What about you?" Jasmine asked.

"What about me?" Victoria questioned.

"Family, friends. Are you in a relationship? Tell me something about yourself. I'm quite sure you're successful at whatever it is you do," Jasmine said as she looked around to add emphasis to her question.

"My mother died, and I inherited a large responsibility. I never had time for anything outside of work. But that's no longer a thing. I'm starting over," Victoria explained.

"Which is why you moved to the United States," Jasmine chimed in.

"Yes, that's it."

"The two of you are exactly the same," Jasmine blurted out.

"The two of who?" Victoria was confused.

"Yourself, and my best friend. You two haven't found each other yet," Jasmine replied.

"What are you talking about?" Now Victoria was beginning to think that Jasmine was a bit crazy. Perhaps Jasmine is the wrong person to show me around the area, Victoria thought.

"Now don't look at me like that. I'm not crazy if that's what you think. Just give me time and you'll understand. Trust me. The universe didn't lead you here by coincidence," Jasmine explained. She stood to her feet, removed her clothes and looked at Victoria.

"I'm not following you," Victoria explained, thinking that this was more of her mad talk.

"You asked me what I saw when I looked at the water. I see nothing but endless possibilities." With that Jasmine dove into the water.

"You're quite the swimmer aren't you?" Victoria asked as Jasmine swam closer to her.

"We were born to be in water. It's part of us," Jasmine replied. She then went further out. Victoria watched her as if she would disappear into the horizon like the setting sun. She knew that one day her life would be defined, and her purpose fulfilled. Whoever thought that money would buy happiness was wrong. Victoria had all of the money in the world, yet she was unhappy. Her life was complicated, and the only person who understood her was Lana who was dead and gone.

* * *

Jasmine admired Victoria for taking the initiative to begin a new journey. Finding herself was Victoria's goal. Jasmine believed that it was all about secrets and whether you wanted to share them or not. And Jasmine chose not to tell Victoria that she was a drug addict. Being a drug addict held a nasty connotation that you had no control over your behavior.

Victoria and Jasmine retired to the living room. Valerie decided to call it a night and left the two of them with an expensive bottle of wine. While Jasmine wasn't much of a wine drinker, four glasses gained favor with her taste buds.

"Why California?"

"California is the mecca of the United States; the place where you find the brightest lights. When I was a little girl, my mother and I often times pretended to be movie stars, and Hollywood was the ideal place for an actress."

"Where's your mother now?" Jasmine asked.

"She died some time ago."

"How did she die?" Jasmine was curious.

"She died of a heart attack."

"What a coincidence. My best friend's mother died of a heart attack as well." Jasmine couldn't believe the similarities.

"What's the odds of that? I guess where there's one, you have two. Whatever that is supposed to mean," Victoria said as she downed the rest of her wine.

Jasmine got up from the sofa, turned the music up, and began dancing around the living room. She moved over to Victoria and pulled her into the action. "Come on," she said. Victoria reluctantly joined her.

Victoria never had any girlfriends to goof around with, and she had to admit that this was quite refreshing. "I need a break now," Jasmine said as she fell to the sofa.

Victoria continued to dance slowly. She closed her eyes and imagined that Lana was twirling her around like she did when they danced throughout the night. It was a long road without her mother. Once she felt like the music had gotten the best of her, she crashed on the sofa next to Jasmine.

"I hadn't done this in a while, at least not in the confines of my own space," Victoria confessed.

"If we're going to go on this journey, you'll have to give me some background on the kind of things that you're into. I must warn you now. I'm quite adventurous. I'm into things that you might not find suitable for your taste," Jasmine explained.

"Try me," Victoria challenged her. The two of them traded ideas on where they should begin their adventure. They spent most of the night lying on their backs and staring at the ceiling.

"I think you should step onto the dock and jump into the water," Jasmine suggested.

"Yeah, sure. That's the easiest way for me to drown."

"Do you believe in love?" Jasmine asked.

"Of course I do, but I feel as if love can be a trap. Placing you with someone or something that can be ripped out of your life at any time."

"That's why you go all in while it's within your grasp. I think the two of us are going to get along just fine. In fact, I'm sure of it," Jasmine said as the two of them closed their eyes.

*　*　*

I wonder how different life would be if you were me.
Lost within yourself,
like unread books hidden on a shelf.

Failed intentions of admirations entangled,
broken hearts discarded and rediscovered
in the lost and found.

I wonder how different life would be if you were me.
To see as I see and be as I be.
To feel alone and divided,
like undecided thoughts that rest within your unsettled
mind.
Endure grinds of land mines that explode and destroy
pain as it unloads.
Only to wonder how different life would be if you were me.

If you were devastated by exaggerated love
that hesitated to love you the moment it gravitated
your way.
Compelled by the untruths,
lies of honesty that deceived me.
Broken to the point that only I believe me,
and finally I see,
life is different for those who aren't really me.

CHAPTER SEVENTEEN

Chanel

It was a make-believe symphony of colors. Red depicted a hot inferno; a yellowish-orange shadowed the sunset as darkened skies controlled the night; and a melancholy blue buried a life of trauma. The injection of heroin hit Chanel hard and fast.

Chanel's body was sensitive to the touch. A warmth between her legs hungered for attention. She slipped one hand into her panties and two fingers into her vagina. The movement of her fingers hurled her body towards an orgasm. But this time, something was different. There was a burning sensation in the middle of her chest; more like a stabbing pain she had never experienced before. The orgasm was replaced by a repulsive act meant to eradicate any desire for pleasure. Vibrant colors turned dull and lifeless, and a fog surrounded her like an impending storm.

The burning in her chest grew. The increased anxiety reminded her of an earlier conversation with her doctor when she had overdosed. He warned her that the next drug overdose could kill her. Teetering on the threshold of a total black out, Chanel reached for her phone. Her vision was foggy making it difficult to see the screen; her fingers shook and life, itself, was about to end. She found the number and hit the call button. Desperate to live, she called the one person that could help her.

I stared into the face of death; the cold, relentless, and dreadful gaze. Death, itself, urged me to come closer, egging me on to follow the dim-lit path to everlasting peace. Life as I knew it, was about to deflate into a life void of all feeling. This was the moment I chose to live or die. Death was permanent, something that I couldn't undo. I was a rebel without regrets and had been gifted and afflicted with life.

Dr. Smith received a phone call in the middle of the night; a call without words. Only the sounds of someone struggling to survive could be heard. Fearing the worse, Smith got into her car and drove to Chanel's apartment. The drive was filled with anxiety over what could happen or what she might see. There was the lingering thought that Chanel might have overdosed and unable to return. Smith had no idea as to why she felt so connected to Chanel. On occasion, Smith had lost control to Chanel, leaving herself in a somewhat dubious situation.

There were times when Smith even had passionate dreams about Chanel and sometimes woke with soaked panties. Her husband even commented about the sensual sounds she made during some of her dreams.

When Smith pulled into the parking lot there was an inner voice telling her to leave. She could be getting into a bad situation, finding herself under Chanel's control. Still, Smith knew that this could be a life or death situation, and she was obligated to protect her client.

Her first knock was light, barely audible. She then tried the doorknob. It was locked. There was a welcome mat at the front door. Maybe there's a key under it. She picked up the mat. No key. She reached her hand above the door trim and found nothing. That's when she noticed the door jam. It was the exact same model of door that Smith had in college. She sometimes locked herself out of her apartment and used a credit card to bypass the lock mechanism and gain access to the room. She removed the credit card from her wallet and looked to see if anyone was watching. She placed the card between the lock and door jam. The door didn't move. She then remembered to push hard against the door.

Smith cautiously stepped inside and called out Chanel's name. No reply. The place was well kept indicating that this was Chanel's apartment. After closing the door, Smith walked into the kitchen and headed towards the back rooms. There was a door slightly open. As soon as she pushed the door open, Smith saw Chanel on the floor; naked and very pale with a slight pulse. To Smith, this was a drug overdose for sure. Smith removed her jacket, ran to the bathroom to draw a tub of cold water. She then raced back to the room and dragged Chanel's body into the water.

"My name is Tianna Smith and I need an ambulance for someone who overdosed on heroin," Smith said as she gave the emergency dispatcher the address.

"Come on Chanel, wake up," she said while smacking her face. But she was unresponsive. Smith raced to the kitchen and removed all of the ice from the freezer and dumped it into the bathtub. Time was not on her side. Smith couldn't do anything but wait.

CHAPTER EIGHTEEN

Victoria

The sun rays slithered through the curtains in Victoria's bedroom. She pulled the comforter over her face. In an earlier time, she would have been out of bed before the sun had an opportunity to awaken her. But now, Victoria's life was changing.

She had a hangover and could only remember having a good time with Jasmine who was passed out in the guest room. Victoria didn't recall making it to her bedroom or getting undressed. While she began to gather her thoughts, there was a knock on the door.

"Come in."

"Sorry to bother you, but we have a meeting with Blake Goldman in a few hours," Valerie said. She handed a glass of orange juice and a couple of Advil's to Victoria.

"Shit, I totally forgot. What time is it?"

"Almost two o'clock," Valerie replied.

"How much time do I have to pull myself together?"

"An hour, give or take," Valerie answered as she handed Victoria a folded piece of paper. "Jasmine left this for you," she added and left the room.

Blake Goldman was an event planner, someone who knew his way around L.A. Once her head cleared she read the folded piece of paper.

I'm glad the two of us were able to connect on such a great level. I had a good time last night and can't wait to continue this journey with you. I'm sorry I had to leave so abruptly. Something came up. You were sleeping so peacefully that I decided to leave you a note instead. I'll be sure to call you at my earliest convenience.

Jasmine

Victoria folded the paper and placed it on her nightstand. Things were different since Victoria began her new journey. Her actions were unrestricted and absent from the scrutiny that held her back in previous years. Gone were the judgements and comparisons between Victoria and her mother. In Canada, her family held a well-known name; a name that resonated with the wealthy and those seeking perfection. Victoria's short stay in the states had been filled with excitement, leaving her with a new-found glow never seen before.

Victoria stood underneath the shower head as it sprayed hot water on her head. Fingers moved through her hair, lessoning the built-up tension in her back and shoulders. If she had her way, she would have remained in the shower for an extended time. But that would have to wait. Victoria stepped out of the shower and walked into her bedroom as Valerie was laying her clothes across the bed for the evening event. Valerie looked up and saw a naked Victoria and quickly turned away.

"What, you've never seen a naked woman before?"

"I'm sorry, I thought you were still in the shower."

"Have you always been this apologetic?" Victoria asked as she proceeded to dry herself.

"I was raised to be respectful." Valerie replied, still a bit apprehensive.

Victoria saw the pencil dress on her bed and instantly thought of her mother getting ready for another outing. Lana had the charm to light up an entire room and hold the audience's attention for the entire evening. She was more sophisticated than Victoria and enjoyed the social affairs that her daughter shunned. As adults, Lana and Victoria's physical appearance was strikingly similar but their chosen paths became quite different. Victoria finished dressing and told Valerie to call their driver.

Victoria sat in the car while her thoughts remained on her mother, and how the two of them were robbed of time together. While she was grateful for the inheritance Lana had left her, she would trade it all just to have more time with her mother.

Playing with imaginary friends and having sleep-overs where pillows were dressed to appear as real friends were the norm. All Victoria knew was what her mother told her and the things she saw through the windows. She would soon learn that to live was to make mistakes, formulate corrections, and develop her moral compass.

*   *   *

Victoria was not disappointed. The venue was massive and elegant, just as she had requested. While Victoria and Valerie walked among the guests, a tall man approached. "I'm Blake Goldman. Nice to meet you." Blake extended his manicured hand and gave them a proper handshake.

"Like wise, I'm Victoria. I really like this space."

"I'm glad you like it because it's what we have and it's nonrefundable. So, what's the look you're going for here?" Blake asked.

"White, anything as long as it is white. Valerie will help you with whatever needs to be done."

"And the budget?" Blake asked as he entered notes on his cell phone.

"There is no budget," Victoria said. She then walked through the double doors that led to a massive water fountain with a rainfall back drop. The massive amount of water that ran through the construction of granite and marble was mesmerizing. There was a look of intrigue on her face, one that Valerie had witnessed when Victoria was near the river. Victoria approached the fountain and noticed the fish that swam beneath the surface. She touched the water and felt the chills that ran up her spine. Victoria did not know that Valerie and Blake were watching her.

"What are you projecting to gain from this event?" Blake asked.

"Nothing less than twenty million dollars."

"That's quite a number. Don't you think we should be more reasonable?" Blake commented.

"Mr. Goldman, you let me worry about the numbers and the people needed to fill the room. I just need you to focus on the moving parts around the event." Victoria spoke with a firm and determined voice. Victoria was throwing a masquerade event to raise money for the Special Effect, a nonprofit organization, with a focus on building schools in urban communities. While Victoria had always given back to the less fortunate, she did not consider herself to be a philanthropist. But the title came with the territory. She wanted to set a precedent for the legacy she would leave behind and finish the work her mother had begun.

"What's the deadline?" Blake asked.

"As soon as possible. If extra time is needed, be sure to check with Valerie for the details," Victoria explained.

"Sounds like a plan. What about money for the materials?" Black inquired.

Valerie handed him a credit card. "There is a $200,000 spending limit on the card. If you need more just give me a call," Valerie said, as she gave Blake a number to contact her.

Victoria and Valerie left in their car and decided on finding a place to eat. Valerie was amazed at how stern and polished Victoria was, especially to be so young. She was a woman that knew exactly what she wanted and how to get it. Valerie had never met another woman who came close to the stature of Victoria.

"What do you think about Jasmine?" Victoria asked.

"She seems nice," Valerie replied. "Why do you ask?"

"I just feel connected to her somehow, and I can't explain why. But something is definitely there," Victoria explained.

"I think you should take your time before jumping into an emotional relationship," Valerie suggested.

Victoria didn't reply. Instead, she looked out the window and closed her eyes and spoke. "Lana had dictated my every move when I was younger. I never made any mistakes on my own; mistakes to learn from. I want to live without a harness, allowed to jump from a building with no idea if there's someone to brace my fall."

"I think you have the desire to seek change, and that is great. But to be reckless is another thing, something that you're not privileged to do," Valerie said.

"And why is that? Because I'm this billionaire with too much to lose, or because of the thousands of people I employee?" Victoria questioned.

"Not just that. But your mother. All that she built would be for nothing if you were to throw it all away. Her death would be meaningless." Valerie hoped that her words reached whatever part of Victoria's brain that dealt with rational thought.

"My mother was lonely. She devoted her life to pleasing people and neglecting herself. I refuse to die the way she did. And if I burn my fortune to do so, then so be it."

Victoria wasn't a woman you controlled or convinced to go against her opinions. She had gotten a taste of what her life could be and living on the edge was more enticing than the safe-zone. Valerie was more reserved and was prepared to offer a more reserved approach if necessary; a constant reminder of the life that Victoria was running from. She wanted to lose control and live without restrictions. Fuck fear and playing it safe. That's how Victoria felt.

* * *

The rain unloaded some six inches of rain in less than an hour. Water raced into the room devouring everything in its path. I stood on the bed watching water move closer and closer. There was no escape. The water covered my tiny ankles and was rising faster than before. My knees nearly buckled as the frigid water circled my kneecaps. I closed my eyes, waiting for the water to go away. When the water reached my neck, the sheer power of the storm strangled me. The water kissed my lips and swallowed me whole.

Victoria bolted from the nightmare, struggling to gather her thoughts. She had no idea why large bodies of water scared her so much. Perhaps it was a fear of the unknown; what lurked beneath its surface. She wanted to jump into the river and force the fear from her body.

Victoria got out of bed and walked into the bathroom to take a shower. Once she stepped from the shower, she sat outside on the patio, looking to see the stars before the sun began to rise. Lana had told Victoria that the stars were different planets; places where people traveled when they died. While there were several imaginary stories, nothing topped *"The Black River."*

CHAPTER NINETEEN

Chanel

A life-support machine was connected to Chanel's body. The drug overdose caused an aneurism to explode near her heart and a swelling around the brain caused a blood vessel to rupture. The pressure surrounding her brain had to be reduced or she would die. Chanel was unresponsive while she awaited her fate. She was in a coma. The doctor remembered that he had told Chanel many times before that she could die if she had another drug overdose. Everyone knew that she was not fond of being told how to live her life. But now it was up to Chanel. Did she have the will to live?

Her psychologist, Dr. Smith, sat in the waiting room waiting to be informed of Chanel's prognosis. Hours passed. Still no information. Smith's mind began to think the worst; imagining that Chanel had died.

A doctor walked into the waiting room. "I'm Dr. Jones, and you are?"

"I'm Dr. Smith."

"Medicine?"

"I'm a psychologist."

"Nice to meet you. Okay, for now she is stable but in critical condition. There is some swelling around the brain, but we can't operate until it subsides on its own. There were ruptured blood vessels near the heart. We were able to remove most of the fluid that leaked into her chest cavity. I'll be frank with you, her situation is extremely dire. Ms.

Rosenthal has been treated in our emergency room more times than I can count for drug related overdoses. I had warned her that the next time she overdosed, she could possibly die," the doctor explained.

"I really don't know what to say," Smith admitted.

"There really isn't anything to say. I'm sorry. You can see Chanel, but don't expect any response." The doctor walked off and left Smith to her thoughts.

The walk to Chanel's room seemed miles away from the waiting room. Smith wasn't sure as to what she could say. There was so much going through her head. When Smith opened the door, Chanel was lying on the bed with a tube in her throat and another in her nose. This wasn't the young, vibrant, assertive lady that Smith knew. The sight of her was heartbreaking. While Chanel was always in control, she was dancing along the shadow of death.

Smith took a seat near the bed and stared at the floor. I wish I could have helped you, Smith thought. There was a cry for help, and I missed it. Why didn't I see it coming? I wished you could have called me like you normally did.

Smith had never felt this connected to a patient. Chanel had a spirit about her that was both empowering and alluring.

"Is she dead?" Jasmine asked as she walked into the room, catching Smith off guard with her presence.

"No, but she's in bad shape. I'm sorry, who are you?" Smith was puzzled. Chanel had never talked about having any friends and here's this woman who looks exactly like Chanel.

"I'm nobody important," Jasmine said and turned to leave.

Smith jumped to her feet. "Wait!" she yelled and then tried to catch the lady. But when Smith turned the corner, she was gone. There were no doors or any place she could have gone. Smith walked back to Chanel's room and saw that her lifeless body was still there.

"I think I'm losing my mind," Smith said and decided it was time for her to get some sleep.

* * *

AN EARLIER SESSION BETWEEN
DR. SMITH AND CHANEL:

"I have this switch that changes my behavior. When the switch is turned off, something, possibly some entity, controls my actions. I have no choice. I just give in. When the switch is turned on, I have power over my decisions," Chanel explained to Smith as she took notes of their conversation.

"I think you're in search of something like I've said before," Smith replied. "Now it's all about finding out what that something is. You're a smart girl, and in time you'll discover the secret," Smith explained.

"I wonder why sex makes me feel whole. I know it's only for a short duration, but I thrive in its presence," Chanel explained. "When the moisture in my panties tingle the insides of me, I become aroused and want to be devoured. One minute my body craves to be high, and the next, it wants to be had. A woman's need to be had is like no other resolve in the world. Maybe it's because we are emotional creatures. I love the feeling when I climax, the orgasm that sends chills throughout my body," Chanel explained.

"I would consider that to be the cravings of a sex addict. Wouldn't you?" Smith responded.

"Come on doctor. When you're with your husband you must feel the need to be satisfied. To be dominated and engaged with passion. Every woman has this desire."

"My husband is modest, and personally, indulging in my affairs is inconsequential," Smith said.

"You have to let go of your inhabitations, be adventurous and welcoming. You're young and beautiful. So why not live a little?" Chanel asked.

"I have ethical obligations and cannot act outside of those guidelines," Smith replied.

"I think we're well past those ethical, moral obligations. Besides, this is about you getting into the head of one of your patients. What better way to do that than understanding the world they come from?" Chanel asked as she noticed Smith's *increased attention to their conversation. This was the Chanel that most people could not deny.*

"Why are you so interested in me?" Smith asked.

"Because we must connect in order for you to understand me," Chanel answered.

"If I agreed to go along with whatever it is you're trying to get me into, it would have to be out of this state where I'm licensed to practice. I can't believe I'm agreeing to this. One last thing. If I go along with this, there are no boundaries. I get to ask you anything I want, and you must truthfully answer me. And absolutely no drugs," Smith added.

"Of course." Chanel noticed the tattoo of a dolphin on Smith's ankle.

"So, you like dolphins?"

"What?" Smith asked.

"Dolphins. Do you like dolphins?" Chanel asked again while looking at the tattoo.

"Oh, it was just some stupid thing I did in college. I just never had it removed because it's a reminder of something."

"Which is?" Chanel pressed for more information.

"When I was younger, my mother and I visited the aquarium occupied by dolphins. They swam to the glass and made interesting noises letting us know that they had been waiting for us to visit them. It was a bonding experience for the two of us. I know it must sound strange, but when my mother died, one of the dolphins died as well. I began buying all kinds of dolphin stuff—t-shirts, pins, and the like. Some said that I was a marine biology freak. The dolphin tattoo wasn't a mistake. It was a reminder of my mother," Smith explained. Chanel appreciated the fact that Smith shared something so personal.

"I guess we're all searching for what's left of our past," Chanel said. She knew what Smith was going through. Life's uncertainties were like the pieces to a puzzle. But sometimes we don't have all of the pieces.

"How did she die?" Chanel asked.

"No one knew. She was here one day and gone the next. The doctors called her case an anomaly, a medical mystery were their exact words," Smith explained. But Chanel thought Smith

was hiding something. People sometimes hid the things that others could scrutinize and pick apart.

"There's a rave this weekend," Chanel mentioned. "I think it would be a great way to understand my world a bit more than asking questions in an office."

"What's a rave?" Smith was clueless.

"Fun!" Chanel shouted.

* * *

The weekend came quickly. Smith was trying to rationalize what she was about to do. Her gut instinct was telling her to back out of it while she still had the chance. But she decided to proceed with their plans. Las Vegas was a city of lights, a place where you were allowed to run wild. You could do whatever you desired, and if only for one night, you were granted that privilege.

Smith had no idea as to what she was getting into. Chanel wasn't into roller-skating or being a bowling kind of girl. She was audacious, perilous, and didn't give a fuck. And she lived on the edge without any concern that her actions would cause her death.

When they arrived at their destination, there was a huge bon-fire. People were jumping around and vibing to the music that blared across the open field. Smith had never seen this kind of organized chaos. They navigated their way through the crowd and ended with some beers and a bench near the back of the lot.

"This reminds me of my college days," Smith yelled over the music.

"That's the point. People come here to unwind. Most of the people are doctors, lawyers, you name it. None of your accolades or work bullshit matters here. Just fun," Chanel explained.

They drank some beers and somehow ended up with a bottle of moon shine. While Smith wasn't a heavy drinker, she thought why not? She gave into the moment and allowed herself to let loose. By now, Chanel and Smith were dancing and being lifted above the crowd. Everyone seemed to connect to a common source of energy. Glow sticks and marijuana bowls were being passed around. Smith indulged without regrets and felt like she was on a cloud. She couldn't recall when she had experienced so much fun. Her husband was basic and borderline simple.

"I'm glad you decided to come," Chanel yelled over the music.

"Yeah, me too." Smith was surprised that she was having such a great time. She wasn't too messed up or incoherent. This was more of a mellow vibe; no drunken blur of acts that she would regret the next day. If this was the worst side of Chanel, then maybe she had her wrong all along.

Smith was all over the place, taking advantage of her night on the town. She let her hair down and whipped it around like a mad rock star. Chanel laughed as she watched Smith come out of her shell. They danced close to each other, grinding and pushing up against one another like life-long partners.

"Look at you all bubbly and worked up," Chanel said.

"I haven't drank like this in quite some time. The water, it's so good!" she said and chugged the reminder of the water bottle. Smith had no idea that the water she drank was spiked with a couple of *Molly's*. The two of them partied until the very last minute and called it a night.

Smith was sweaty and exhausted by the time the two of them made it back to the hotel room. Chanel knew that Smith had a good time. Life wasn't about work and Smith needed a break from fixing people.

"I had such a good time," Smith admitted and collapsed onto the sofa. Chanel was already on the other sofa. They were borderline drunk, and not ready to call it a night.

"My husband would go nuts if he was to see me like this."

"Good thing we're away from the distractions and you're able to let loose." Chanel said.

"I'm glad I was able to see the other side of you. You're so full of life and energy. I wish I still had it in me to be adventurous."

"You're still young. I know you have a husband and the job, but happiness is possible. Why work hard your entire life and not feel happy at the end of it? Some people never discover what makes them tick," Chanel explained as she stood.

"Don't be afraid to take chances." With that, Chanel headed to the shower. While standing in the shower, Chanel felt a cool breeze sweep through the room. She turned around and saw Smith standing naked. Words held no meaning at this point. Chanel embraced Smith's body. Her skin was warm and soft and alluring, and the passion could be felt everywhere.

Chanel kissed her neck multiple times in a slow cadence that moved on to her breasts; the movement of a carefully composed symphony. Chanel pinned her against the wall and slipped a finger inside of her vagina. Smith let out a breath of air and welcomed her touch. Chanel removed her fingers and tasted her sweetness. The two of them moved on to the second movement where each phrase melted into the next. Smith opened the shower door and stepped out.

"You coming?" Smith asked. Chanel followed. The two of them slid onto the satin sheets as their naked bodies shared the passion that had directed their emotions. Their tongues locked together into the deepest part of their mouths while Smith inserted her fingers inside of Chanel, pushing downward with each thrust of her fingers. Her vagina was sloppy and heavy with juices, indicating that a climax was about to be had.

By now Smith had her hand buried inside of Chanel, followed by a rush of fluids from Chanel's body. She then pushed Smith onto her back and parted her legs. Pleasurable sounds escaped Smith's mouth as she grabbed a hand full of Chanel's hair.

The eruption of orgasmic explosion caused Smith to roll over and clasp her legs shut. Chanel forced her legs apart and climbed in between her legs in a position where their vaginas touched. Chanel closed her eyes and slowly grinded until the friction from Smith's snatch was wet and pleasurable. She pinched her erected nipple and opened her eyes to see Smith's face. With wrinkle brows and a clenched jaw, Smith came again. The two of them climbed each other for as long as their bodies were able to climax. Once they were consumed by exhaustion, they took another shower and retired to the bed.

Chanel couldn't sleep. She was troubled by where her life was headed. Hours later, she turned her attention to Smith who had settled down for the night. While Chanel wished this could last forever, she realized that it was not a likely outcome. Smith had been seduced and conquered by Chanel's charm. This one night was merely an escape from Smith's boring and predictable life. Chanel closed her eyes and fell asleep.

CHAPTER TWENTY

Dr. Smith

I never thought that I would find myself in such a compromising position. I was a licensed psychologist committed to separate my personal feelings from interactions with my patients. Despite all of my training, I was unable to keep myself from acting human.

Dr. Smith visited Chanel on a regular basis, hoping that someday things would return to normal. The doctor said that Chanel's condition was bad, and that there wasn't anything he could do at this time. While Smith's practice was not her main concern, it kept the lights on. Life was frozen in time, waiting for Chanel's status to change.

Smith walked into Chanel's room and replaced the flowers that she'd brought a week earlier. The nurses reminded Smith that talking to Chanel could stimulate her brain activity.

"I wish you were awake," Smith said to Chanel. "Having to deal with so many patients is driving me insane. My husband thinks I need counseling. I think he is having an affair, and I honestly don't give a shit," Smith explained.

"Excuse me," the doctor said as he entered the room.

"I'm sorry," Smith said. "I was talking to Chanel, hoping that it would help."

"Please don't be sorry. You're doing what's necessary in order to help a loved one," the doctor replied. The mention of a loved one caught Smith by surprise. He was assuming that Chanel was someone close to Smith. Was she? That was the question in Smith's head that made the most sense. Maybe she should consider Chanel to be a loved one.

"We're considering putting her in our out-patient program. There's no good way to say this. Chanel is showing no signs of improvement and she has no insurance. If you have a place for her to go, we can have our medical staff come and set-up the equipment. Ms. Smith, this is going to be quite a journey and will require lots of effort on your part. While I'm not saying to give up, I'm warning you that it might seem impossible," the doctor explained. Smith's silence was an indication of the magnitude of her problem.

"What will happen to her if there's no one willing to take her in?" Smith asked.

"I'm afraid she will be taken off life support."

"That's it? All because she has no one, her life isn't important. How can that be legal? You people should be ashamed of yourself," Smith snapped.

"I understand your anger, but this call isn't up to me. The board of directors make these kind of decisions. I'm just a doctor assigned to the patient."

"How much time do I have to make a decision?" Smith asked.

"Thirty days. From there you can request an extension of time which might buy you an additional forty-five days. I can delay the process for you and make things drag out a bit. So, let's just say that you have six months," the doctor explained.

"Thank you," Smith said. "I'll get on top of things right away." The doctor smiled and walked out of the room. Smith's stress level had just gone through the roof. She had no idea who to contact for Chanel. She couldn't let her die as if nothing happened. But how could she get away with bringing a complete stranger into their home? Just then, Smith had an idea. But first, she would have to figure things out from a financial standpoint. Smith stood over Chanel and looked at her.

"You'll owe me big time after this. And I really mean big time. You have to wake up because the world is due for a laugh." Smith touched her hand and left the room.

*   *   *

AN EARLIER THERAPY SESSION
BETWEEN CHANEL AND DR. SMITH:

"Sometimes I feel trapped in my own head and I can't get out of it. I feel as if I'm being consumed by my thoughts," Chanel said as she closed her eyes and told Smith how she felt.

"As I've told you before, you have to learn to get out of your own way and doors will begin to open. You're very intelligent. I just feel like you're unable to deal with yourself," Smith replied. Writing notes for Chanel's sessions weren't needed for future sessions. Her issues were always the same. Chanel was an adrenaline junkie who thrived on being challenged by dangerous acts of indecency; her heart needed to be pushed to its limit; and boredom would cause her to self-destruct.

"You really think I'm screwed up, don't you doc?"

"I believe you're searching for something in particular, so if that qualifies as being screwed up, then we're all messed up," Smith responded.

"The man who raped me was diagnosed with a terminal cancer. I watched him die an agonizing death. I sat in front of his bed and smiled until my face hurt, knowing that he was suffering — dying on the inside."

"You still haven't talked about that part of your past."

"Jeffery Smith."

"That was his name?"

"He was quite the man if you asked me. Charming, thoughtful, and someone that you could depend upon," Chanel explained.

"How does that make you feel today, knowing that he deceived and violated you?"

"Disappointment, rage, hurt and betrayal. But none of that matters anymore. I chose not to relive the past. I live my life as if there's no tomorrow," Chanel responded.

"That can be dangerous."

"Life is dangerous. Why not just give into it? Be free from the fear of dying." Chanel got up from the sofa and walked to the window. She saw a bird sitting on the edge of the window frame. The bird had an array of colors running through its feathers. And the eyes, they were blacker than coal. Something caused Chanel to open the window and reach for the bird. When she tried to grabbed the bird, her body almost toppled over the rail. Smith ran to her and grabbed hold of her shirt before she went over.

"Are you trying to kill yourself?" Smith yelled.

"I was just trying to grab the bird. It was right there," Chanel attempted to explain.

"There was no bird," Smith said as she walked Chanel back to the sofa. Smith had never seen Chanel this shook up, and for the first time, Chanel seem scared.

*   *   *

Chanel had no idea where she was. Her mind was trying to make sense of her surroundings. She looked around and saw bright lights overhead. There was no one in sight. When she made her way down the hallway, there was a nurse sitting behind a desk. She then knew that she was in a hospital. The lady smiled as Chanel approached the desk.

"Can you tell me where I am?" Chanel asked.

"You're in St. James General Hospital," the nurse replied. Chanel had no idea what she was doing in a hospital, but it had to be for some reason. She immediately considered the possibility of a drug overdose. And maybe that was the reason she didn't remember anything.

"By chance, do you know why I'm in here?"

"Room 321. You're a visitor," the nurse replied. "Don't worry, I get tired and forget things as well."

Chanel walked from the desk to room 321. But along the way, a little girl in a nearby room waved at her. Chanel stopped and returned the wave. The girl called Chanel into her room.

"What's your name?" the girl asked.

"Chanel, and yours?"

"My name is Casey. The doctor said that I have to stay here, but my mother said that I can come home soon."

"Why are you here?" Chanel asked.

"I have leukemia, and when I'm done with my treatments, my hair will grow back, and I will be pretty again."

"You're already beautiful baby doll. And you'll beat your leukemia. If I were you, I wouldn't worry about my hair. You're beautiful with or without your hair."

"Thank you," the little girl said. Chanel held Casey's hand and noticed that she was no more than fifty pounds in a very fragile body. The slightest movement could break her body in half. Chanel saw the unfairness that Casey was forced to fight for her life before it had begun, and to do so without knowing whether tomorrow would ever come.

"You can go see your friend now. She needs you," Casey said.

"What are you talking about? What friend?" Chanel was confused.

"The girl that looks like you in room 321. The one with the pretty smile," Casey replied. Chanel said her goodbyes to Casey and left the room heading towards room 321. She had no idea what was going on nor what she was walking into. Chanel was still trying to sort through information to determine why she was in the hospital and who was in room 321.

It was late in the day and the medical staff was between shifts. The hospital gave off a strange feeling, like the place was abandoned and isolated from the world. Chanel began to feel the hairs on the back of her neck stand in an erect position. Once she entered room 321, she suddenly stopped. She tried to prepare herself for what was on the other side of the wall. Chanel took a deep breath and opened the door and walked inside the room. Her heart pounded hard, each movement required her total strength.

Except for the beeping sounds of the life-support machine, the room was quiet. When Chanel approached the bed, her knees buckled; her heart rate accelerated; tears ran down her face; and a lump in her throat shut off her oxygen supply. She grabbed hold of the wall for support.

"This isn't real. This isn't real. This isn't real," Chanel said to herself. Her mind was confused and petrified when she saw a manikin-like body stretched out on a metal slab. The body was that of Dr. Smith. This made no sense. Why was she in the bed connected to a life-support machine? Chanel did a quick scan of the room and refocused on the woman. She was gone. Smith was no longer the woman on the slab. Instead, it was Chanel's body in a coma, unresponsive and barely alive.

Chanel's soul drifted above the table searching for her physical body lying on the bed. Would her soul wander off to another place, a place unseen by the living? Or would she live to see another day?

CHAPTER TWENTY-ONE

Victoria

The flight back to Canada seemed longer than before. For Victoria, the dark, gloomy day would never end. The man she knew as Mr. Butler was the closest thing to a father she had ever known. His death squeezed the life from Victoria and suffocated her soul. Mr. Butler was the one person in her life that was always available. Even during the times when her mother was emotionally inaccessible, he was there.

Victoria had grown used to the different culture in the United States. Now that she was back, she would likely become reacquainted with the continuous cycle of madness hidden in the veil of organized chaos.

The driver pulled up to the estate that Victoria had known as home. This was the place where the memories of Lana's fondness and gentle ways evolved. At the same time, the estate seemed more like a prison that prevented her soul from evolving in the open sunlight. She felt the pain hidden beneath the decorated chandeliers and expensive fixtures.

As Victoria walked through the double doors, time seemed to stop. She looked towards the staircase hoping to see if Mr. Butler would help her with the luggage. She closed her eyes, knowing that unwelcome memories were about to surface. Victoria gathered her things and headed up the stairs to the room she called her sanctuary; the place where pain, grief, and acts of discontent were not allowed. Victoria knew that one day she would have to return, just not so soon. The two people that she had loved were gone. Victoria was all alone.

"Can I do anything?" Valerie inquired as she searched for the right words to say.

"Not at this moment. You can go see your family. I've got things from here."

"Are you sure?"

"Quite." Victoria assured her. Valerie noticed the sadness in her eyes and questioned whether she should go. Perhaps she should remain by her side. Valerie felt it best if Victoria planned Mr. Butler's funeral. Now Victoria was left to think about her life and the fact that there was no one to carry out her legacy. While many believe that money brings happiness, Victoria knew that success has meaning only when you have someone to share it with.

Victoria climbed into bed and drifted into a steady gaze. She stared at the mountain of stuffed bears in the corner of her room that had functioned as her imaginary friends throughout her childhood. Victoria's thoughts were interrupted by the rang from her phone. It was Jason. He was grateful that she gave him the company and allowed him to be his own man. Victoria was appreciative to have Jason around as well.

"Are you alright?" Jason asked.

"I'm fine. I just have so much to deal with at this time," Victoria replied.

"If anyone's up to the task, it's most definitely you. I wish I could change the outcome of a lot of things, but I don't think the world works like that," Jason explained.

"Sadly, it doesn't. I'm sitting in the house trying to gather my thoughts and figure out what needs to be done. I just need time to think. It sucks being in this house by myself and have no one but my depressive thoughts," Victoria explained.

"I can come over if you like," Jason suggested.

"I wouldn't ask you to come down to my world of misery. I think it's enough with just me having to deal with it," Victoria replied.

"I wouldn't mind. Besides, that's what friends are for."

"I can't promise that you'll enjoy my cooking," Victoria said.

"Of course I wouldn't enjoy your cooking," Jason answered as Victoria laughed.

"You can darken this threshold at your own will," Victoria warned.

"I'll take my chances," Jason replied, adding that he would be over in an hour. She ended the call and went back into her head searching for an escape from the painful revelation that she would be burying another person she loved. The world was so unpredictable. Victoria had no idea how to move forward.

Jason's family was close to Victoria's grandparents. Over the years, Lana had built a relationship with Jason's family. He was a couple of years older than Victoria. The two of them often conversed whenever their families got together. Victoria knew that Jason had a crush on her, but nothing went beyond that. He was a good looking guy and the perfect partner for someone like Victoria. Although he had a massive crush on her and often vocalized his admiration, nothing went beyond his innocent flirtation.

The doorbell rang and Victoria went to let him in. She'd just gotten out of the shower and her hair was still wet. She wore a pair of cut-off shorts and a tank top with no bra.

"I came bearing gifts," he said, holding up some Chinese food.

"So you mean to tell me that the feast I just prepared for the two of us is now a waste?" Victoria asked with a look of disappointment that could be quite intimidating.

"I'm just kidding," she said while grabbing the food from his hands. The two of them sat on the sofa in the living room and turned on the television.

"There's something that seems different about you," Jason said. "I can't wrap my finger around it." He removed the chopsticks from its package.

"I only wonder what that can be?" Victoria replied with a wink.

"How are things in the states?" Jason asked.

"They're both interesting and eventful. While it takes some getting used to, I'm enjoying it." Victoria admitted. She got up from the sofa and retrieved a bottle of wine and two glasses from the cellar. She then returned to Jason and filled both glasses with a rich, red wine.

"How are the numbers?" Victoria inquired.

"They're as expected. Business is better that I projected. I'm just learning the business a bit more, but the timing of it is all great," Jason explained.

"See, I knew you would land on your feet. You just needed a little nudge," Victoria said as she playfully pushed.

"I still think having you around is good for the morale of the company," Jason admitted.

"Good for the company or you?" Victoria shot back.

Jason was used to her bluntness. But seeing this side of her was something new, something he'd never seen before, and something that fueled his desire to be with her. His hunger for Victoria was strong and did not go unnoticed.

"What have they done to you in California?" he asked.

"They made me more dangerous, like mass-murder dangerous," Victoria joked.

"I can say this for sure. I miss having you around and knowing you're only here for a short period of time is the reason I'm here right now."

"You make it sound as if I'm going to disappear from the face of the earth and never return," Victoria responded.

"Knowing you, it's not impossible," Jason replied with a smile. His face was clean shaven; his hair was well groomed; and his rugged, bad-boy persona and favorite wine contributed to Victoria's feelings of arousal. But the silent stare from her eyes made him feel a bit uneasy.

"Are you alright?" Jason asked while downing the rest of the wine.

"Why wouldn't I be?" Victoria got up from the sofa and pulled the tank top over her head, exposing her erect nipples. Jason had a bewildered look on his face.

"You don't just have to sit there. You can join me." Victoria's aggressiveness disarmed him of all assertion and he instantly became submissive. When she wiggled out of her shorts and slid her panties down, Jason's mouth watered with eagerness. He froze with uncertainty, trying to read her facial expression to determine if she was serious or just playing around.

It became obvious that Victoria had the same lustful intentions as she moved closer to Jason. She sensed his heart pounding with anticipation. While he was nervous, he wanted nothing more than to be in the moment. As Victoria placed her hand on Jason's chest, she felt an immediate erection bursting through his pants. Their lips met, transferring a warmth from her body; enough to drive him crazy. They responded like life-long lovers as their kisses became wetter. Victoria felt his erection pushing through the fabric of his jeans and was impressed.

Still, Jason was having difficulty processing the changes in Victoria and questioned whether this was real or a dream. His curiosity mixed with her passion created a favorable blend. When Victoria began kissing his neck, Jason knew this was real. As he picked her up and carried her to the sofa, they began shedding clothes immediately. He had never seen Victoria like this. Her conservative nature and coyness she had possessed were gone.

While the size of Jason's penis was a bit intimidating, Victoria was up to the challenge. She pulled Jason in between her legs as he gently pushed his penis inside her wet vagina. Her body tensed up as his penis fully entered her body. While Victoria was in a state of euphoria, Jason was being careful as if she was a porcelain doll.

"Harder, harder. Please go harder," Victoria moaned. Jason obliged as each stroke produced more intensity. Victoria went from a loud moaning to a high pitch scream. Jason stopped and looked at her.

"Am I hurting you? We can stop." Jason asked with concerns.

"In a good way. Keep going," Victoria responded. He picked up where he left off, continuing as if this would be their last night together.

Victoria began to challenge his sexual advances from the bottom as she rocked back and forth. Her nails dug into his back while she bit into his shoulder blades. Her body was on fire, feeling like she was about to explode. Her body began to shake. He knew that she was about to have an orgasm. He unleashed all of his power creating a struggle for Victoria to either pull away or continue wanting more. She then came, allowing the juices to lubricate his shaft. Victoria pinched her nipples as the friction provided by her fingers created a powerful arousing.

Victoria's mind drifted elsewhere for a moment. She imagined Jason was Jasmine. She pushed him away with her feet.

"I want you to taste me," Victoria instructed. She then grabbed a handful of Jasmine's hair and arched her back as a bolt of electricity surged throughout her body. She had her legs spread as wide as possible as Jasmine continued licking every inch of her being. When Jason came up for air, Jasmine was gone. Victoria wasn't finished. She had Jason lay on the floor and mounted his erection. She engulfed the full length of his penis and felt him deep into her stomach. She wanted to live in this moment forever.

Jason grabbed hold of her small waist and held on as she skillfully rode him in circular motions. While her vagina was swollen, she was about to explode. He looked into her eyes and noticed how her eyebrows nearly touched as she exploded in pleasure. She bounced up and down on his shaft searching for the last ounce of her orgasm.

Jason couldn't hold back any longer as he exploded as well. The warm semen made her even more aroused, causing her to collapse onto the floor. Both of them were exhausted from consuming each other.

*   *   *

Victoria soaked in the bathtub as she speculated that her life would never be the same.

Mr. Butler was one of her closest friends and now he was gone. Mr. Butler and Lana had been ripped out of her life, torn away like the final two pages of a worn-down novel. Lana had taught Victoria that you could create your own world to live in; design things to your liking; and fashion all aspects of life to fulfill your desires. The thought of playing God within your head is one thing, but reality is an entirely different realm with no boundaries. Uncertainty is measured by assumptions, not really knowing, but still moving forward with the notion that things are as they should be.

Now that Victoria looked at the reflection in the mirror, she realized the person was a stranger. Victoria's life had been arranged and created by Lana, and her brain was hardwired to stay the course.

Victoria stepped out of the tub and proceeded to dry herself. While doing so, she watched the water in the tub as it circled down the drain. She was mesmerized by its sheer power and presence. Water could not be destroyed, only contained in some instances. Something clicked in her head. She got dressed and headed to the pool house and turned the lights on. She stood at the edge and watched how the lights at the bottom lit the water, giving it this illuminated glow that appeared warm and inviting. A body of water can draw a person in, causing them to dive into the unknown. Victoria wasn't naive, she knew the looks of it was a ruse. Most things of a deceptive nature have the ability to lure you in.

Victoria inhaled a large gulp of air and noticed the grimness that filled her nostrils. Water released the smell of death. But today was different. Victoria was done being a slave to her fear of drowning. Today she stood up for herself, and the cost was of no concern. She closed her eyes and jumped into the water. She descended straight to the bottom of the pool. It wasn't what she thought the water would be — frigid, dark, and petrifying. It was quiet, calm, and inviting.

Victoria opened her eyes and noticed a blue, cloud-like landscape that spread everywhere. While she was caught up in the moment, the beauty and solitude of the water world, she forgot about the life-sustaining necessities like oxygen and her inability to swim. She tried to kick her legs and swing her arms but couldn't move. The water moved like quicksand, pulling her down, further down. Her lungs fought hard to maintain enough air supply to survive. Although her mind was willing, she couldn't compete with her physical inabilities to survive. She couldn't swim.

She went from being calm to a state of panic as her oxygen supply was depleted. Drowning was no longer an imaginary thought; it was a reality. She saw black spots as her brain was shutting down; drifting off as a loud splashing sound was heard up above.

* * *

To most people, I was a suicidal, nut-case for jumping into the pool and not being able to swim. There was no logical

explanation that satisfied the "saner ones." I was tired of
running from my fears in ways that kept me from embracing my
potential. Since drowning was my largest fear, it felt right, at the
moment, to challenge the thing that threatened my wellbeing —
diving in the water while not knowing how to swim.

I had no idea how Jason found me in the pool house. He
saved me from myself and prevented me from being dragged into
a lifeless spiral. Although I was still alive, my mind knew that
I had died when I jumped into the pool that night.

I was wrapped in a bathing towel with my knees held tight
against my chest; still shaken up as I danced along the shadow
of death. Jason was frightened as he pulled my body from the
water. He looked at me, trying to make sense of my senseless act.
For him, there were no words to express the disappointment he
felt. What could he say?

While Jason didn't want to seem insensitive, he needed answers. "Are you trying to kill yourself or am I overreacting?" he asked. Victoria had this stale expression on her face, appearing to be in an alternate reality.

"I have no idea what is going on in your head." Jason stated as he raised his voice. He took a seat next to her looking to show support. Victoria's silence was not helping. "The least you can do is to tell me that you're alright. Is that unfair for me to ask?"

"I'm not your problem." Victoria finally spoke.

"And that's all you can come up with? I just fucking saved you from drowning. If I wasn't curious as to why you weren't in bed, you would be dead." Jason spoke out in frustration more so than anger.

"I never asked for any of this," Victoria shot back. "You decided to jump in after me. You got what you wanted from me, so why do you care if I live or not?" Victoria's words cut deep.

"If I want to jump in front of a bus, I can do so. It's my life. I don't recall you being here when my mom died. All I have is the man I'm here to bury." Victoria continued her rant as tears cascaded down her cheeks. She wasn't looking for any kind of sympathy nor to be someone's pity case.

"I got what I wanted. You think this was about sex? Fuck you Victoria. I'm sorry I wasn't there when it counted, but I'm here now." Jason shot back.

"Just leave me alone." Jason wished he could do something to help. All he wanted was for her to be happy. Victoria was emotionally unreachable at this point. While he wanted to break down with her, he had to be strong for the two of them.

"I'm heading home. If you need me just call." Jason walked away feeling helpless. He felt as if his heart had been ripped from his chest. He loved Victoria, but he had to leave before one of them said something that they could never take back.

Although Victoria didn't mean it, she had said some hurtful things. She wished there was another way for her to vent. Now she had to live with her actions, hoping that he would forgive her one day. Victoria stood up, stretched her legs, and walked around the estate to clear her head. She needed someone to talk to.

"Mr. Butler," Victoria yelled as she quickly realized that he was gone. The one place that was supposed to be home was toxic. Victoria felt the energy being squeezed from the estate's foundation; the agony falling from the walls; and the depression seeping through the floors.

Perhaps the fear of water was a distraction from the real problems in her life. Maybe she hadn't dealt with her mother's death. Instead of mourning the death of Lana, she had to deal with the death of Mr. Butler. Victoria felt like everyone had abandoned her. As she was lying in bed, there was a rumbling in the sky. She slid out of bed and opened her window to welcome the sounds and sight of a raging rainstorm. The wet-earth and the smell of water-soaked grass reminded Victoria of running through the lawn with her mother. There was something magical about Mother Nature's on-going dance with the environment. As the rain continued to fall, Victoria whispered to the sky, "I'm sorry you are sad."

Victoria decided to go outside and run in the rain. It was her way to unwind from all the built-up stress. The sky caused Victoria to move from sadness to a giddy, child-like behavior, reminiscent of an earlier time. The memories took her back to simpler times before life had become ugly. Now she understood why Lana had sheltered her from a world filled with disappointments and painful memories.

Victoria laid on the grass and looked upward into the heavens, hoping that an angel would take her to see her mother and Mr. Butler. She flapped her arms as if she was making a snow angel, hoping to be saved. With eyes closed, she enjoyed the moment; the roar of the thunder; rain beating against the house; and gusting winds that howled like a pack of wolves. And then, without notice, everything went silent as if God had hit the pause button. Victoria opened her eyes. The rain was gone; the winds were still, and her hair and clothing were dirt dry. Lana left the world as a broken woman, someone who never found love, just hurt and misery. Victoria walked into the house and broke down into an uncontrollable crying spell. Victoria was alone. Jason was her only friend and now he was gone.

*   *   *

While Victoria was exhausted from feeling sorry for herself, she hated not being in control of her emotions. Sadness was replaced with rage; expensive paintings were flung to the floor; glass tables, lamps, and anything in her path were smashed. Victoria's screams were loud and violent, a protest to the heavens for placing her in a chaotic world. During the midst of her emotional breakdown, her chest tightened. The ringing in her head had mutated into a full-blown migraine. Victoria managed to grab hold of her phone and call the one person who would save her.

"Sorry, I didn't mean to wake you," Victoria said to Jason.

"It's alright, what's wrong?" Jason asked.

"I don't want to be alone. Can you come over?"

"Sure, I'll be there in a second," Jason said as he hung up the phone. While Victoria admired Jason for being a good friend, she loved him for being so understanding. She smiled, knowing that he was on his way.

*   *   *

Funerals are a reflection of the person about to be buried. I looked around and saw a few people who knew Mr. Butler. Others in attendance appeared to be actors hired for a photo-shoot. While I intended on having a small gathering for Mr. Butler's funeral, more people reached out as a sign of respect. But still, I have to admit, I think some people can put a smile on their face for a camera and in an instance, go back to caring about themselves while ignoring others. I allowed one of the maids who held a deep friendship with Mr. Butler, to speak at the funeral.

Even at the grave site, I saw people squeeze a tear or two from their eyes while hiding their true agendas. Mr. Butler was a man who I thought would live forever; a man who was in control of his emotions while maintaining an infinite amount of wisdom. He practically raised me and taught me to be a free thinker. The world had no idea what kind of man they'd lost. We watched in silence as his casket was lowered into the ground. I closed my eyes, realizing that he was gone, never to return. Jason held my hand.

CHAPTER TWENTY-TWO

Dr. Smith

While Dr. Smith had devoted her life to the care of her patients, meeting Chanel was a game changer. There was a spiritual and unworldly energy that connected the two of them, causing Smith to question why she had become so caught-up in Chanel's world.

While Chanel was still in the hospital, no explanation had been provided as to when and if she would wake from her coma. Although Smith prayed that she would, hope and reality were two different conclusions.

Smith stepped from the shower and reached for a dry towel. She thought back in time about the woman who taught her everything about psychology, social development, and the overall psyche of the human mind. Smith made a mental note to contact Kathy Clark who might provide some emotional stability to her life.

Smith arrived at the hospital for another day of hope and prayers that Chanel might wake from her coma. As she walked into the room, Smith wasn't certain as to whether she was entering a dream or not.

"Surprise!" Chanel yelled.

"You're, you're awake?"

"You sound disappointed that I'm back from the dead."

"It's not that. It's not that at all. Your condition was deemed critical and you've been in a coma for some time." Smith paused, still unsure if this was a dream.

"The coma was like an out-of-body experience. I met this little girl who had cancer. This little girl who was unusually wise and spiritual, told me to go see my friend before she was gone. So, I went to room 321,and when I crossed the threshold, the woman in the bed was not me, it was you. And then, in a flash, it was me," Chanel explained.

"I don't understand," Smith replied.

"You told me while I was sleeping that you had no idea how you allowed me to gain control of your will; how you needed me to recover; and how you'd fallen in love with me," Chanel explained.

Smith knew this to be true. She spoke those words to Chanel, and she meant them. But Smith didn't have the courage to admit this to the conscious version. Chanel knew that Smith wasn't one to admit to things that made her feel uncomfortable.

"Ms. Rosenthal. Oh I'm sorry, I didn't know you had company. Good to see you Dr. Smith." The doctor said as he entered the room. "Now, back to you young lady. I can't explain your miraculous recovery and why you are alive and well before my very eyes. I reviewed your chart. The test we ran on your blood came back clean. It appears as if nothing was ever wrong. To be certain, we'll run you through a few more tests and a CAT scan. Then you'll be free to go," the doctor explained.

"How could that be possible? I mean, she just spent weeks in a coma, and now there's no problem?" Smith inquired.

"Dr. Smith, I've been practicing medicine for more than 35 years. Ms. Rosenthal's case is beyond her being lucky. It's a miracle. I have no explanation as to what has happened here." He then turned his attention to Chanel. "If you have no belief in God, you should now." When the doctor left the room, Chanel sat up in her bed. Smith was still at a loss for words.

"How did I end up here?" Chanel asked.

"You called me, and when I made it to your place, you were unconscious," Smith explained.

"You saved my life," Chanel said.

"I wouldn't say that. Maybe I helped you in a time of need. This is a lot to take in. Sorry if my answers don't make sense," Smith replied.

"Has anyone been to see me besides you?"

"No," Smith replied while seeing that something was on Chanel's mind.

"Why do you ask?"

"I was sure that Jasmine would have been here. At least once to see if I was fine." Chanel appeared sad because her best friend had not been to see her. Smith has never seen Jasmine in person, but she knew a lot about her from previous sessions with Chanel. It seemed like the more Smith knew about Chanel's world, the more she was pulled along for the ride.

"I think I'm going to run. Run until the emotional upheaval ends," Chanel said.

"Run away from what?" Smith wanted to know.

"Everything. Everybody. I think I'll end up dying if I don't. I have this feeling like I'm sinking into this dark hole. I don't know who I am. Maybe that's why I'm so carefree in my actions."

"Taking things a day at a time always helps," Smith said. "On the bright side, your hours in my office are complete, and I'm out of your hair." But Chanel smiled, knowing that the facade of wanting out wasn't real. Smith was tangled in her web and had no way of escaping.

"We can never be finished doc. The fun has just begun. Besides we have things to figure out."

*   *   *

While Dr. Smith drove in silence, she was disturbed and unsure of her next move. She failed to tell Chanel the many things that they had in common. Chanel's mother had died and the man she called father, had sexually assaulted her throughout her younger years. Smith and Chanel were broken, looking for someone to save them. As they stopped at the red light, Smith looked over at Chanel who was asleep. She looked so innocent while filled with so much life. Her possibilities were endless if given the chance.

"Do you see me?" Chanel asked while her eyes were still closed.

"I thought you were asleep," Smith replied.

"I've slept enough. If I fall asleep, I'm afraid I will never wake up. I want to get high so bad. I can taste it and feel it running through my veins."

"Are you serious right now? Chanel, you almost died but by the grace of God you still alive. And you're still talking about using again?" Smith questioned. She then pulled over the car and turned to face her.

"I'm not here to lecture you nor dictate any demands. I'm here because I genuinely care about you. You need some help, and if you give it a chance, you'll be on your way to recovery," Smith promised.

When Chanel didn't reply, Smith grew angry. "Do you want to die? If so, you can get out of the car right now," Smith shouted.

"I'm willing to take some help, but I'm not going to any rehab center. If you want to help me I'm more than willing," Chanel negotiated.

Smith looked at her and shook her head. "You're a hand full, you know that?"

"So I've been told."

CHAPTER TWENTY-THREE

Jasmine

For weeks, Jasmine had been looking for Chanel. She called the local hospitals, known associates, and anywhere the two of them had been. She wanted to call the police and file a missing person's report but chose not to. The last time she had seen Chanel was after a yacht party. Jasmine left the following morning to meet up with a friend. It was like Chanel had dropped off the earth.

"I don't get it. Where could she be?" Jasmine asked Victoria.

"Maybe she's out on a date or with some friends. Just give it some time. I'm sure she'll appear from the shadows." Victoria played it down trying to relieve some of the stress in Jasmine's mind.

"So, what's she like?" Victoria asked. "I know you told me, but I'd like to hear it again."

"Chanel's a mystery. Someone who isn't an easy read. It's like I unlocked her in a way. I broke into her mental hard drive and found a part of her that had never been discovered."

"Sounds like you know her well," Victoria commented.

"I want to show you something," Jasmine said as she walked her to the mirror.

"Okay, what now?"

"As I describe her, I want you to tell me who you see in the mirror."

"Alright," Victoria replied.

"Her eyes appear dark, like they are hiding a secret. You can see the youthfulness in her features. Her innocence hangs on as the turmoil from a hard-life rages on; her lips are full and pink like the inner layer of your gums; and her Carmel-colored skin has a smooth texture. Who am I describing?"

"You're describing me," Victoria answered, feeling a bit surprised.

"No, I'm describing a part of you. I'm describing Chanel." Jasmine explained while Victoria's face wrinkled up with confusion. Being that this wasn't the first time that Jasmine referenced the two of them — Victoria and Chanel — as being two-in-one, Victoria thought there might be something wrong with Jasmine.

"What do you mean?" Victoria questioned.

"Give it time. It'll make more sense at a later time. So, how was the funeral?" Jasmine asked.

"It was fine, just depressing. But I'm glad it's over." Victoria admitted.

"I think most funerals are that way, but it's a necessary problem to endure. I'm glad you asked me to come over. I was bored out of my mind."

"Welcome to my world. Boredom is my culture," Victoria said with a sarcastic remark.

"We need to fix that fast. So, where's your friend Valerie?"

"Valerie works for me. She's tending to those things back in Canada. I'll be opening an office in Los Angeles soon."

"What kind of office?" Jasmine asked.

"I own a capital company that deals mostly in stocks, bonds, and other securities. We also provide a line of capital to large corporations."

"Sounds too complicated to me. Speaking of work, I have an audition for this play called *Falling*. While it'll be on one of the largest stages in California, the play will ultimately land on Broadway," Jasmine explained.

"I didn't know you were an actress," Victoria remarked.

"Well, not so much an actress. I'm more of a dancer, ballet and contemporary. Yes, I know. Most people wouldn't believe a girl of my caliber could be involved in a dance so sensual."

"I wish I could dance. It's like I have two left feet," Victoria joked.

"You should come. I'd love to have you in the auditions cheering me on."

"I'd love to be there. When is it?" Victoria inquired.

"It's next week."

"Just give me the time and place and I'll be there," Victoria assured her.

Jasmine was hiding something that Victoria felt was important. Victoria knew there had to be a secret within the confines of her brain. Friendships shouldn't be constructed with lies and hidden secrets. Victoria wanted Jasmine to know that she could be trusted, and there was no reason to put up barriers. But she understood. This world was complicated and filled with so much anger. Diablerie was recycled and thrown back into the ethers like plush clouds.

Victoria fell back to sleep, appearing to be out for some time. Jasmine seldom slept. She was unable to rest through the nightmares that haunted her each night. Jasmine stood over Victoria and watched her sleep as if she didn't have a care in the world.

"I know your secrets but they're safe with me," Jasmine mumbled while walking to the window. The rain began falling from the sky, causing Jasmine to smile. She placed her hand on the window.

"I'm sorry you're sad," Jasmine said.

CHAPTER TWENTY-FOUR

Dr. Smith

Chanel's skin was soft. I felt myself becoming aroused by the thought of what she was doing to me. I could not determine if her touch was so powerful, or if it was the thought of doing something wrong that was so enticing. Either way, I enjoyed it. Hearing Chanel share her stories of sexual escapades were intoxicating. I bit down on my pen to distract me from rubbing myself. The moisture in my panties was evidence that she had turned me on. I rubbed my knees together so the fabric of my panties would create some friction that burned below. I was controlled by a woman that was broken in so many ways.

Smith turned in her sleep, moving her body from one side to the other. Her silk pajamas rubbed against her erect nipples. Mark, her husband, was awaken by her moans of pleasure accompanied by movements that nearly pushed him onto the floor. Her nightly salacious acts had become more frequent. Mark was puzzled by the dreams that she experienced. He chose not to wake her, deciding to watch, hoping that she might call out a name. Smith's hands found their way into her panties as she began to finger herself. The room began to smell like sex, the scent that came from below. She arched her back, followed by a major orgasm.

Mark couldn't deny his anger and the jealousy that his wife could have been dreaming about having an affair. But he was turned on as well. The erection in his boxers were evidence of that. She suddenly opened her eyes and noticed that her hand was covered in nectar. She didn't notice that her husband was watching her from the other side of the room until he spoke.

"Must have been a hell of a dream," Mark said. Smith was so embarrassed that she didn't provide a reply.

"You've been having these wild, sexual dreams a lot lately. I don't know who you are anymore. Tell me, are you having an affair?" Mark demanded to know.

"Don't be an idiot. You know damn well that I'm not having an affair," Smith shot back. She got up from the bed and pulled the sheets off as Mark hurled additional accusations.

"Tell me what is going on. We haven't had sex in God knows how long, and all of a sudden you're having these sexual dreams. Do my concerns sound unreasonable?"

"I just have a lot going on right now. It has nothing to do with you."

"It's affecting our marriage. Can't you see that?" Mark explained.

"Mark, I'm not having an affair, and if you're feeling like our marriage is being challenged, then maybe you should look at yourself." Smith shot back.

"And what is that supposed to mean?"

"I haven't been happy in years. But you've never noticed because you're not home enough to do so," Smith yelled.

"Maybe we should consider other options." Mark was angry.

"Don't be indirect with me, Mark. Say what you mean. Be a man for a change and own up to what you are feeling," Smith shouted back.

"Be a man. Is that what you said? I want a divorce. Is that man enough for you?" Mark replied as he stormed out of the room. Smith didn't bother to go after him. Instead, she headed to the shower.

TWENTY-FIVE

Chanel

Chanel and Jasmine sported matching bathing suits at a yacht party arranged by Jade Reed. One night earlier, when Chanel was working as a bottle girl at club BED, she was approached by Mr. Reed, a famous actor and public figure with connections to powerful people around the world. Jade invited Chanel to a yacht party to be held the following night. While Chanel never mixed work with her personal life, the right suitor sometimes initiated a breaking of the rule.

Chanel wasn't star-struck by the famous. To her, they were people with a lot of money accompanied by too many cameras flashing at the most inappropriate times. While she accepted the invitation, she wouldn't dare darken the door without Jasmine, her long-time partner in crime. Unlike Chanel, Jasmine was a different story. She sometimes fantasized about being rich and famous, imagining the thrill of being recognized by the entire world.

Chanel and Jasmine's imaginary plan was to make an appearance with the hope of being found naked and passed out on the beach of some foreign country.

The party was hosted on two yachts connected by a walkway and located near the Golden City, a piece of land carved out for the wealthiest of Californians. Jade Reed was most definitely part of that company. Jake's family owned their own television network which helped Jake become one of the highest paid actors in Hollywood. It could be said that he had a head start in life, and from there, everything fell in place.

The moment Chanel and Jasmine stepped onto the yacht they were surrounded by waitresses carrying trays filled with drinks and delicious appetizers. There were scores of available men and beautiful women waiting to connect. It didn't matter your social status, everyone was having a great time.

"Chanel, right?" She heard someone call her name. It was Jade Reed accompanied by two beautiful women.

"I see you're good with names," Chanel said.

"Not many. Just those who catch my eye and leave a lasting impression."

"That's a classic line for a movie star," Jasmine chimed in.

"And you are?"

"The girlfriend!" Jasmine replied with a little attitude. The look on Jade's face was priceless, leaving him at a loss for words.

"I'm just joking. I should have been an actress myself. I'm the bestie," Jasmine said while extending her hand.

"We're glued to the hip. She's my partner in crime," Chanel added.

"Well in that case, it's nice to meet your partner in crime. I'm glad you could join us."

"Like wise."

"Would you ladies care to join me below deck?" He inquired. Once they agreed, Jade sent the other women away. The trio navigated through many sections of the yacht until they came upon two marble doors leading to a room furnished with a large flat-screen television that hung on the wall, casual furniture, a pool table, and a massive 500-gallon fish tank with an assortment of sea creatures. The people in the room were well into the party atmosphere.

"Fellas this is Chanel and Jasmine. Ladies, these are my good friends, John Walsh, the movie producer, Ed, the Banker, and Johnny Davidson who owns the company that films most of my projects." As Jake introduced the guys in the room, Chanel's mind drifted elsewhere. She didn't care too much for the men in the room. There were buckets of ice and a mountain of cocaine on the table. Chanel was surprised that men of such caliber wouldn't be more discreet about their personal life, especially if it involved drugs.

Chanel found the party setting to be quite refreshing. She could be herself, and not have to pretend to be someone else for the sake of gelling with Jade's entourage. They sat on the sofa and wasted no time joining the party. There were drinks and coke on plates passed around like cocktails in a night club. The music set the vibe and the people moved to the beat.

The cocaine was pure in quality and quick to take hold of your mind. Ecstasy was just a snort away.

Jasmine was quick to stand on the table and sway her hips back and forth to the music. Most men ogled her, imagining the joy of being inside of her. Adding Chanel to the mix was pure sexual torture to a man's state of mind. Jasmine grabbed Chanel's hand and pulled her onto the table where they grooved into sensual movements. The other women in the room were taken back by Chanel and Jasmine's flaunting ways. There were no inhibitions or boundaries; the two of them danced together as if no one else was in the room. Jasmine walked the length of the long table and took the bottle of expensive scotch from one of Jade's friends. The man was in a trance as he studied Jasmine's hypnotic ways of reeling in a man's attention.

"Are you enjoying yourself?" Jasmine asked Jade.

"I most definitely find the two of you to be entertaining," Jade replied.

Jasmine took a drank from the bottle and passed it on to Chanel.

"Entertaining sweetie?" Jasmine said. "You haven't the slightest idea of who you're dealing with. Trust me on that," Jasmine added and then went back to dancing on the table.

"Your trouble," Jade replied.

"Then get out while you can. Run, run, and run fast." Chanel warned. Jade smiled and looked her square in the eyes.

"Running isn't my thing. I'd rather deal with what's to come," Jade assured her.

Chanel and Jasmine inhaled the majority of the coke, showing no sign of slowing down. While high, they were still coherent. Jasmine let loose; swinging her hair and grinding to the music. While the other women in the room could not complete with Jasmine and Chanel's energy, they went to a different part of the yacht.

Jade wasn't much of a dancer and chose instead to watch their moves on the dance floor. By now, the majority of the people had left, leaving Jade and the waitresses who he chose to send home. The yacht was empty. He walked back into the room where Chanel and Jasmine were drinking and getting wasted.

"I see the two of you had a good time," Jade said as he took a seat across from them. Jade was a good looking man in his mid-thirties with a muscular built. His piercing eyes drew women in like a Cobalt magnet. While Jasmine kept her eyes on Jade, she pulled Chanel's face to hers. The two of them kissed while fondling each other's breasts. Chanel and Jasmine knew every inch of each other's bodies and knew what buttons to push. Chanel removed Jasmine's top and licked her pierced nipples. Jasmine slid out of her bottoms while Chanel's fingers found their way inside of her.

Jade pulled his penis out and began stroking himself. By now, the ladies were completely naked while licking each other in passionate ways. They moved over to join Jade on the sofa. Jasmine pulled his jeans off while the two of them got on their knees. Chanel took Jade in her mouth as Jasmine tasted his lips. This was the world where they maintained control and absolute power; the world where women reigned over men.

Chanel rubbed herself and ignited a flame that burned throughout her entire body. She felt the effects of the cocaine tingling through every fiber of her being. The foreplay had worn out its welcome and was begging for the ultimate orgasm. Jasmine mounted Jade's penis and rode it slowly. As Chanel held Jasmine's face with both hands, Jade was holding back the buildup of his orgasmic explosion.

"Your turn," Jasmine told Chanel as she released herself from his penis. As Chanel got up, she saw Jade's glossy and lubricated shaft. Jasmine pinched Chanel's nipples and began kissing her neck. She was more interested in Chanel than Jade.

Just like a jealous lover, I knew that Jasmine would want more of me, and that I could never deny her. We were soulmates, connected by vines of energy from a different realm. I often times wondered how Jasmine and I had cheated fate and broke some kind of unforeseeable chain of events by being together. We were meant to be together in a different lifetime, but somehow, we found each other in this world. We shared an unimaginable love found in a yet to be named planet.

Jade was on his feet with Chanel positioned on his shoulder and pinned against the wall while he continued licking her pussy. Jasmine was on her knees devouring every inch of his erection. She welcomed the challenge of making his knee's buckle from her skillful sexual prowess. Just when he felt weak at his knees, he pulled away and got some laughter out of Jasmine. Chanel was lowered and replaced by Jasmine being bent over the sofa. Her vagina was so wet, Jade reached the bottom of her tunnel in one stride. She looked back at him and pushed herself back towards his advances. Her moans made Chanel wetter and aroused to the point where she needed to feel something inside of her. She opened her legs and fingered herself at a high speed. Jasmine and Chanel locked eyes while Jade pounded on the walls. Thinking about Chanel brought Jasmine to an immediate orgasm. Jade grabbed Chanel's waist and stroked her with long strides. He pounded her harder until they both came and collapsed on the floor.

"I think I need a nap," Jade said.

"You'll need more than that," Chanel replied as she and Jasmine began getting dressed.

"Where are you going?" He asked.

"We don't do overnights when it's the two of us. We sleep alone. This was fun. Maybe we can do this again sometime," Chanel suggested as they said their goodbyes and left Jade to himself.

CHAPTER TWENTY-SIX

Chanel

*Perhaps some people thought I was dead, possibly in a ditch
or at the bottom of a lake. Or maybe I was out of sight, out of
mind. While some might think that I'm fucked up and a bit
unstable, that doesn't mean that I'm a bad person. I've fucked
married men, stole, and done a shit-load of drugs. That's who
I am, that's what society made me — a survivor. I've died a
few times, and sure, I can tell you about the white light you
see when crossing over. It's quite euphoric to be honest. But the
most exhilarating things begin that way, offering just enough to
draw you close; close enough to sink their fangs into you. Then
the fun and games are over, and you're left to pick up the pieces.*

Chanel was sitting on the sofa while eating junk food and watching
cartoons in a house Dr. Smith had inherited from her parents. Chanel
heard a car door slam shut. When Smith opened the front door, she was
carrying a bag and suitcase.

"You going somewhere doc?" Chanel asked.

"I had a fight with Mark, and as of last night, we're officially
separated and filing for divorce," Smith said as she collapsed in the
recliner.

"I'm sorry to hear that, what happened?" Smith didn't respond. She
was thinking about her dreams and the sexually vivid thoughts that

ran through her head. Chanel's sexual journeys were trapped inside of Smith's head and continued to drive her crazy.

"We had a big argument. Things were said and we decided it was time to go our separate ways." Smith didn't provide Chanel with the whole truth. She didn't want Chanel to know it was initially due to her dreams and how they sexually aroused her in ways that Mark was unable to do.

"You sure you don't want to talk about this?" Chanel asked.

"I'm tired and need to sleep," Smith replied while closing her eyes.

Chanel walked outside near the river and placed her hands in the water. The current pushed the water between her fingers. She stripped down to her panties and bra and dove into the river. The water was like a giant canvas where each stroke of her arms painted a portrait. Besides drugs, this was the one place that opened her mind to other thoughts.

While not having Jasmine by her side, swimming in the river was the best thing she could do at this time. Jasmine kept her grounded and offered an element of excitement to her life. Perhaps it was time for a change if she wanted to live.

Chanel swam to the bottom and sat on the river's floor, hoping the calm water would help her recover from the years of abuse. While her lungs needed air, Chanel tried to ignore the urge and remain on the bottom. Finally, she forced herself to the surface and got out of the water. She then walked into the house and checked her phone for messages. The call that grabbed her attention was from Gerald Day, the man who escorted her to the masquerade party in Canada where she met Victoria. Chanel was curious and decided to make the call.

"Mr. Gerald Day," Chanel said the moment he picked up the phone. "Sorry I missed your call. I was out back swimming darling."

"That's alright. How have you been?"

"The usual. Eventful is the best way to describe it."

"So, I received a call a few days ago from Ms. Victoria Bloom. Do you recall meeting her during our previous trip to Canada?" Gerald asked.

"The rich girl. Yeah, I remember her. Why do you ask?"

"Apparently she has been trying to make contact with you for some reason. I told her that I would ask you to give her a call," Gerald explained.

"I have no idea what she would want with me, but I'll give her a call." Gerald gave Chanel the telephone number and the two of them talked for a few minutes before ending the conversation. There were a million thoughts running through her mind as she wondered why Victoria was looking for her. Their meeting was brief and nothing more than a casual conversation. Chanel dialed the number and waited for Victoria to answer.

"Hello," Victoria said.

"May I speak to Victoria?"

"This is she."

"I hear you've been trying to find me, rich girl." In that instance, Victoria knew it was her. Who else had ever referred to her as rich girl.

"In fact, I have spent a great deal of time trying to track you down and here you are."

"I'm curious to find out why, and I'm certain that you will tell me," Chanel replied.

"I have something that belongs to you — a dolphin pendant."

"I thought I would never see it again. My mother gave it to me when I was a little girl. I'm thankful for your determination in tracking me down. You can mail it to me. Canada is out of my reach at the moment," Chanel explained.

"I'm here in the United States. California to be exact."

"Oh, that's great. I'm in Los Angeles," Chanel replied with an air of excitement.

"It looks as if fate is on our side. We're in the same city. I have some business to attend to, but once I'm done we can meet somewhere," suggested Victoria.

"Sounds like a plan," Chanel replied.

"I'll give you a call at my earliest convenience."

"I'll be waiting."

* * *

*The winter storm clung to the Chicago landscape like a
Canadian Goose Parka on the coldest day. The blistering winds
pierced most any fabric during this storm in this place called the
Windy City. The playground was occupied by several children
who ran around as if it was a summer day. While they mingled
about throwing snowballs and building a larger than life snow
fort, there was one child who remained isolated from the group;
a child who the group often times made fun of. On this day,
there were two children who bullied her.*

"Leave her alone," Chanel demanded. The girls turned to see who
had addressed them.

"Or what? What are you going to do about it?" One of them
challenged.

Chanel approached the girls and got into their face. "We can find
out if you like," Chanel replied in a stern voice. The girls backed off as
Chanel helped the girl to her feet.

"Are you alright?" Chanel asked.

"Yeah, thanks," Jasmine replied.

"No problem. You have to stand up for yourself and stop letting
people bully you."

"I'm not a fighter," Jasmine answered.

"And you don't have to be, but you have to stand up for yourself,"
Chanel explained.

"I guess you're right."

"Here, take this." Chanel handed her a small pocketknife. "If
anybody fucks with you while I'm not around, you use it," Chanel
instructed Jasmine. She placed the pocketknife in her pocket and
smiled. Chanel knew that she was weak, but in this world you have to
be tough. And Chanel would teach her that.

"Where are you from?" Chanel asked.

"Everywhere. I was moved around a lot and did some running
away," Jasmine explained.

\"You got a name?"

"Jasmine!"

"Nice to meet you Jasmine. I'm Chanel." The two of them shook hands and became inseparable.

Chanel was more assertive — the risk taker — while Jasmine became her loyal pupil. There wasn't much to do but get in trouble, and that's exactly what the two of them did. Under Chanel's guidance Jasmine came out of her shell. Being juveniles, the system tried to find foster care for both Chanel and Jasmine. While not wanting to be separated, they intentionally sabotage interviews with foster parents. They showed temper tantrums and crazy-like behavior, and even acted as if they were possessed by \demonic spirits; anything to avoid being separated.

Two years had come and gone. The child transition center was about to close due to financial reasons. As a result, all of the children were going to be scattered throughout the city in different institutions. While Chanel and Jasmine considered running away, the winters in Chicago discouraged them from doing so.

One day while the two of them were sitting in front of the child transition center, a nice looking car pulled in front of the center. The car was more luxurious and that spelled money. Going with a family that had money might not be that bad, the two of them thought. The family ultimately decided to adopt Jasmine. The fact that Jasmine was leaving was heartbreaking for both. Any twelve year old would be torn from the loss of her best friend.

"We can run away and never come back," Jasmine said as tears ran down her face.

"We have nowhere to go," Chanel explained. "I don't want you to regret this later. Besides, you will be going with a rich family." She could tell that Jasmine was scared and Chanel felt helpless. This was against everything that the two of them had pledged — we will stay together forever.

"Follow me," Chanel said. They headed to the room. Chanel packed some clothes in a book bag and told Jasmine it was time to go. They were about to run away when they made it to the basement. Chanel stopped.

"Shit," Chanel said.

"What's wrong," Jasmine asked.

"My necklace. I forgot my dolphin necklace that my mother gave to me."

Chanel gave the book bag to Jasmine and told her to stay put. There was no way that Chanel was going to leave without the pendant. Chanel's mother gave it to her before she died. It was all she had left that meant something to her. Chanel found the necklace and on her way back to the basement, there was a purse hanging on the door to the head mother's door. Chanel opened it and stole all the money out of it and a bag of marijuana. The duo took off and had no idea where they were going. As long as they were together, that was all that mattered.

*   *   *

While Smith was sleeping, Chanel left in her car and drove around looking for a place to score. She was in agony from the drug withdrawal. She hit rock bottom. She drove around in this foreign area looking for someone that might be a user or dealer. She felt like her body was shutting down and her heart was ready to give away.

Chanel decided to pull over and unravel, to lose it right where she was. She was crying while beating on the steering wheel. Her life was a mess and she wanted out. Chanel had reached her breaking point. How could there be a God that allowed her to go through this pain for her entire life? Being strong all of the time was not easy, and at this moment weakness wasn't something she needed. Chanel pulled herself together and drove to the house. The minute Chanel walked into the house, Smith was upset.

"Where have you been? I was worried sick about you and ready to call the cops."

"I went for a drive," Chanel replied. Smith just looked at her, studying her body posture and eyes. She then approached her to see if her pupils were dilated. She grabbed her face to get a good look and Chanel pulled away.

"I'm not fucking high," Chanel said as she plopped onto the sofa and closed her eyes.

"I wanted to get high so bad. I went looking and couldn't find anyone. So, I came back here."

"Sobriety isn't easy but if you want to live it's necessary. You have to go through this and give yourself a fighting chance," Smith explained.

"When I was younger, I lived in this old house that made sounds as if it was alive. It was a spooky place and I always had trouble sleeping. The doors squeaked and the floors cracked and popped with the slightest pressure. That house held so much bad energy. My memories of that house are plagued with misfortune, anger and grief; a place that I would never want to visit again," Chanel explained.

"Is that where it happened, where your father raped you?" Chanel closed her eyes and pulled her knees to her chest and smiled,

"I remember that day as if it happened yesterday, and my mind plays it over in fine detail. You never forget those kind of things. You just learn to live with them."

"I'm sorry." Smith replied with a tone of sadness.

"Aren't we all?" Chanel replied and smiled again.

"My mother was abusive and extremely possessive. I had to be perfect and chase her failed dreams instead of my own. The world can be a lonely place when you're aiming to please those around you. My mother was bitter, and her passing was a relief." Smith offered a piece of her childhood so Chanel wouldn't feel as if she was being treated like a patient.

"We're the same after all. Just fucked up and broken in different ways," Chanel explained as she stood up from the sofa and removed all of her clothing. Smith was surprised as she watched. "I need a shower." Chanel left the room and headed for the shower.

> Our eyes are the same,
> like we see things together.
> Lost within ourselves
> as imaginary people take shape.
> Our heart awakens,
> still beating at the same pace.

Troubling thuds pound and await
the coming of another form and shape.
She is you, I am her.
We're all the same,
but different in ways that set us apart.
But I see you as you see me,
she sees us through shades of darkness.

Reality crashes the world we saw,
the altered realms that fascinated our minds,
and illuminated our attempts to merge as one.
Now she's gone
and I have vanished.
The time we managed to be together,
be here and gone.
Now it's just you.

CHAPTER TWENTY-SEVEN

Victoria

Victoria's cell phone rang as she came to a complete stop. She recognized the number and answered before the light turned green.

"I'm at your house, but you're not," Jasmine said.

"I have to meet someone. Sorry I didn't give you a heads up. You can leave if you want or just hang out at my place."

"I think I want to continue my adventure of finding you. But this game is getting old," Jasmine said.

"Game, what are you talking about?" Victoria replied.

"And of course you play oblivious — bravo!" Jasmine answered. Chanel was used to Jasmine's troubling statements being hurled about as riddles.

"I'll see you once I'm done with my meeting." With that, Victoria ended the call.

When she pulled into the parking lot of the small cafe, she took a moment to gather her thoughts. She hadn't seen Chanel since their brief meeting in Canada.

"Okay, let's go Victoria," she said as she readied herself for the meeting. Except for an elderly couple sitting at the counter drinking coffee and a creepy-looking, bald-headed guy reading a newspaper near the window, the Cafe was nearly empty. Victoria got a table and removed her jacket to make herself comfortable.

"Can I get you anything?" A waitress approached with a small notebook and seemed surprised when she saw Victoria.

"Wait. Weren't you just here, like 15 minutes ago? You changed your clothes," the waitress asked. Victoria assured her that she'd never been to this restaurant before. While the waitress wasn't convinced, she let it go.

"I'll just take a coffee with..."

"Honey and milk with a raisin bagel on the side," the waitress finished writing the order down before Victoria could complete her sentence.

"How did you know that?" Victoria asked. Now she was confused.

"Because you ordered the same thing earlier, but you were never here," the waitress said as she chuckled and walked away. While Victoria was confused by the conversation, it had a familiarity to it, as if she had said it before. Still, Victoria shrugged it off. She looked at her watch and saw that Chanel was running behind. The waitress returned with her order.

"Enjoy your morning." The waitress said with a slight smile. Victoria thought about leaving but decided to wait a bit longer. Maybe Chanel was held up in traffic or lost. Either way, she didn't want to miss the meeting with Chanel.

While Victoria was engaged in her private thoughts, a bird flew onto the window ledge where Victoria was sitting. While there was something about the bird that was familiar, Victoria thought she might have seen this bird, or one like it, sometime ago. She got up and headed outside while still looking at the bird. She turned the corner and there it was still sitting on the ledge by the window. As Victoria approached the bird, it wasn't intimidated by her presence. She reached out to the bird and it gently sat in her hand. Victoria smiled.

"Hey you," Victoria spoke as if the bird could understand her. Victoria smiled and gently rubbed its head.

"Are you alright?" The waitress came outside and asked.

"Yes, I just wanted to get a closer look at this bird."

"What bird?" the waitress asked. "There is no bird."

"It's right here," Victoria said as she extended her empty palm. Victoria was embarrassed and at a loss for words as she walked back inside. She left a tip and headed out the door. When she threw her coffee cup away, there was another one in the trash just like hers and a partially eaten raisin bagel.

Victoria ran to her car and pressed her head against the steering wheel and closed her eyes. Victoria questioned whether she was going crazy. Nothing made sense. The phone rang. Victoria answered it.

"I'm sorry I couldn't make it to the cafe. Something came up. I tried to call but couldn't get through," Chanel explained.

Victoria didn't say anything. She wasn't sure if she should speak.

"Hello, are you there?" Chanel asked.

"Yeah. I'm here." Victoria finally spoke.

"Can we make arrangements for another time?" Chanel asked.

"Yeah, we can do that," Victoria replied.

"Again, I'm sorry for not giving you a heads up that I couldn't make it." Chanel explained.

"Don't worry about it," Victoria answered.

"Well, I have to go. I'll see you soon."

"Alright, take care." Victoria ended the call while feeling quite confused. She had no idea what was going on, and for the first time in her life, Victoria felt like she needed some professional help.

A week had passed since Victoria had heard from Chanel. While she called her multiple times, no one answered. It seemed like Victoria's life was swept away into a continuous loop where interactions were repeated over and over. Her mind seemed cluttered with a swarm of like-minded individuals, making it difficult to separate herself from the others. It reminded her of an earlier time when people talked in unison, and 2 equaled 1.

*   *   *

People in the audience applauded the dancers who performed on stage. The music was dysphoric, melancholy, and yet fascinatingly enthralled, while the contemporary dance and ballet movements were poetry in motion. When Jasmine took the stage, dressed in a white gown and a make-shift halo that crowned her head, she drew Victoria's attention. The lights grew dim as a single spotlight followed Jasmine's every move, and the music that played at an andante tempo carried her gracefully through her routine. Each measured movement told a tale of an angel who fell from the heavens only to be enticed by the vanity and the laws of an uncivilized world; a presence of sadness; and a soul pleading to be pulled from the misery and disdain. Victoria sat in a trance-like emotional state, feeling the unimaginable sadness release tears from her eyes. Those in attendance applauded Jasmine's ability to tell the story of a broken soul.

Once it was over and Jasmine left the dancer's room, she walked up to Victoria. "How did I do?" While excited, Jasmine was emotionally drained from the performance.

"Splendid, you were marvelous."

"I'm glad you were able to make it. I really am."

"So what now?" Victoria asked.

"They will have a discussion amongst themselves and from there, the finalist will be notified. Fingers crossed," Jasmine added with a glimmer of excitement in her eyes.

"How did your thing go?" Jasmine asked.

"Things?" Victoria was confused.

"You told me that you had to meet with someone last week, and that it was important."

"Oh, it went well." Victoria lied while trying to sound convincing. "I've been a bit forgetful lately."

"Yeah, haven't you!" Jasmine said while grabbing her gym bag. The two of them left the building and went out for dinner. Victoria felt like the two of them had known each other forever. But now, Victoria needed to clear her head and get some sleep.

*　*　*

Victoria had never seen her mother so fragile. She always thought that Lana was invincible, and more than capable of getting through anything. Now she seemed worn down and lacking the strength to carry the weight of her body. Seeing her mother in this condition brought a great deal of pain to Victoria.

Lana smiled as she opened her eyes and saw her daughter sleeping. She loved Victoria and devoted her life to see that Victoria would be financially independent when she was gone. Victoria looked up and connected with her mother's gaze.

"I see you're finally awake sleepy head," Lana teased.

"I didn't realize that I was out. How are you feeling?" Victoria asked.

"I'm fine. Don't you worry about me," Lana replied.

Victoria was used to her mother being proud and stubbornly ambitious. Her valor and audacity to be strong was heartwarming. Lana had been bed ridden for nearly two months with Victoria by her side.

"Pardon my interruption, but it's time for Ms. Bloom to take her medication," Mr. Butler said as he walked into the room with some pills and a glass of orange juice on a tray. The doctors were unable to say how a healthy woman in her mid-forties could deteriorate so quickly and not know why. Victoria hated the possibility of losing her mother, but it was a real possibility.

Unlike when Victoria was a child, Lana couldn't hide anything from her. Although she was a teenager, Victoria was well beyond her years.

"I don't want you to let yourself drown in my circumstances. I want you to be happy and live your life," Lana explained.

"I am, but some things are easier said than done. Besides, you're talking as if you're about to die. I know things will get better," Victoria claimed.

"Tell me one thing. Are you trying to convince me to attend one of your lavish rich-people parties. If so, I think I have the perfect dress," Victoria said and got a chuckle from Lana.

"Of course not. You're too precious to mingle with that class of people," Lana joked in return. "Promise me that you'll find peace with my departure. Don't lose yourself in grief. Life is too short to die before living," Lana explained and began to cough uncontrollably. Victoria jumped up and went to her aid. "I'm fine," Lana responded.

"I'm calling the doctor." While Victoria grabbed the phone, Lana stopped her.

"Remember what I told you," Lana said while letting go of Victoria's arm. Victoria called the doctor and told him that her mother needed help. She held her mother's hand and closed her eyes. Lana's grip became limper while struggling for each breath of air. As the moments passed, Victoria felt a part of herself drifting away. Lana's hand fell to the side of the bed as Mr. Butler walked into the room and pulled Victoria away. The doctor entered the room and could tell from the site of Lana that she was gone.

"I'm sorry," the doctor said. The emotional grief tore through Victoria's body when she realized that her mother was dead. While Mr. Butler tried to console her, he knew that the only cure for such a loss was time.

*   *   *

I remember when I was 14 and experienced the awakening of my sexual desires. It began the night when I heard screams coming from my mother's bedroom. These were not the kind of screams released by excruciating pain. No, these were the screams that accompanied sexual pleasure. The door to Lana's room was not fully closed, allowing a beam of light to escape the room. I slowly moved up the stairs and approached the bedroom door. As I peeked through the lighted-crack, I saw my mother on top of a man that I had never seen before. I knew that she had been dating Todd, but this was a different man.

Lana's face was crinkled as sweat dripped from her chin. I couldn't stop watching as my mind recorded the emotional reactions she experienced, emotions to be sorted out at a later time. Watching the things that my mother did changed the person that I became. My young mind was propelled into a world filled with passion, lust, and deep sexual desires. By the time I had reached 15, the urges led to the touching of my body; exploring it as if I had a mental map of instructions in my brain. By age 18, I took advantage of one of the young men who worked as a landscaper for our estate. I became fully addicted and a slave to my sexual desires.

*   *   *

Each time Victoria heard mourns carry throughout the house, she climbed up the stairs and studied her mother having sex with a man. Victoria touched herself and imagined that she was the one under the warm body. When Lana left the house, Victoria slipped into her bedroom and looked in the drawers for vibrators and other sexual toys.

By the time Victoria had reached 21, she had become a full-fledged nymphomaniac, and had slept with the majority of the landscaping crew who cared for her lawn. When Lana died, Victoria's sexual addiction had increased; so bad that she couldn't go to sleep without touching herself. Being that she never dealt with the death of her mother, Victoria's mind replaced the grief by having meaningless sex, which, in turn, enabled her to feel some level of love.

*   *   *

I felt you deep inside me,
filling my womb with your heat
as I grasped the satin sheets.
Bodies in unison we are,
burning through the pastures of our desires.
Wanting more friction to keep it going,
to keep the fire of passion burning.
Slowly devouring your shaft with wet lips,
originating from deep within my mouth.
Eager to please your advances,
increases the chances of swallowing your soul.
As the walls crash around us,
nothing else matters.
Nothing in the moment goes beyond
the divinity of my dire trinity.
The lustful intentions of my heart,
pound away with anticipation.
Slowly waiting to be undone,
under the clouds through the summer sun.
Screaming out as my soul awakens,

but there's nothing there.
I lone for something to hold me,
to mold me and shape my desires.
Fuel me before I die,
lest I die of a broken heart.

CHAPTER TWENTY-EIGHT

Smith

Kathy Clark, an elderly professor of psychology, had been Dr. Smith's mentor throughout her early career. Smith oftentimes referred to Clark as the one who taught her everything that she knows. While Professor Clark was well established in the world of psychology, her writings are still being studied throughout many Ivory league colleges. Being young and ambitious, Smith gravitated to Clark at their first introduction. Kathy Clark practiced psychological science and the consuetude of Elan Vital; the study of dementia and the human psyche. Some said that she could read a human's psyche and unlock the unknown.

Smith rang the doorbell and moments later Professor Clark answered the door. Smith's initial reaction was that her former mentor looked the same; long platinum hair and high cheek bones and a natural and non-threatening appearance that made her easy to talk to.

"What a surprise Dr. Tianna Smith. How have you been?" Clark greeted her with open arms.

"Quite well, and how about yourself?"

"Graceful and still alive. So what brings you here?" the Professor asked.

"Help, I need some help for a friend of mine and you're the only one that can do so."

"How can I be of service?"

"I don't know exactly. She is quite the adventurous and if we don't find some answers soon, she might die."

"We all have answers that we are in search of, but death does not automatically accompany a journey in search of answers. You can find them and still travel a darkened road," Clark explained while taking a seat. "Tell me more about this friend of yours."

"Well, she's young, adventurous, a drug addict, assertive, and I must say, extremely sexual. I'm having a hard time getting a read on her," Smith explained.

"She's more than a friend and you've actually treated her?" Clark knew the answer before she even asked. Smith reluctantly admitted the truth that it was a cardinal rule to never develop a personal relationship with your patients.

"How long were you treating this woman before you built a personal attachment?"

"I don't know," Smith replied.

"How did the attachment come about?" Clark asked. Smith didn't answer right away. Clark studied Smith's body posture and how she looked down to her left in search of a logical answer. Smith was trying to hide something.

"How is your personal life and marriage?" Clark asked.

"What does my personal life have to do with anything?" Smith questioned.

"I'm just asking questions," the Professor explained.

"I'm going through a divorce and things outside of that could be better as well," Smith admitted.

"You're still going through treatment?" Smith had never shared with anyone, not even her husband, that she suffered severe psychological issues. Clark didn't personally treat her because of the conflict of interest but had sat in on many of her sessions years ago.

"My treatment was completed some time ago," Smith replied.

"I see." Clark was beginning to put the pieces together.

"Wait. What are you thinking? Are you thinking that I'm the one that needs help?" Smith stood while raising her voice.

"I'm just asking questions Tianna." Clark explained.

"No, I think you're working me." Smith remarked.

Clark tapped her pen against the arm of the chair, creating a constant thud that caught Smith's attention. Smith eyes grew heavy as the tapping intensified. "What are you thinking right now," Clark asked.

"Water. I can hear rushing water like its filling a room," Smith explained.

"Why is there so much water filling the room?" Clark asked.

"I don't know."

"Where are you?"

"I think... I think I'm standing on the edge of a riverbank." Smith's body began to shake. "I'm not by myself," Smith added. The shaking increased. Although Clark wanted to dig deeper, Smith's health was more important. Clark snapped Smith out of her trance.

"What just happened? Did you perform a hypnosis on me?" Smith felt betrayed and angered.

"You're still sick Tianna, and you're off your meds," Clark stated with a concerning voice.

"You don't know shit!" Smith yelled as she gathered her things.

"I'm only trying to help," Clark replied.

"Yeah, sure you are." Smith stormed out of the house and never looked back.

*　*　*

> Some people say we are creatures of habit; falling into a routine of emotional highs and lows with a heavy dose of despair. While I used to be happy, the days oftentimes moved like hard mud. I was never meant to be a standout in a crowd of people or the main character of a life story. Perhaps we should take a second look at what life was meant to be; what is true and what is an illusion.

"You seem a bit disturbed," Chanel said to Smith while watching her drift into a daydream. Smith snapped out of it and rubbed her face.

"I'm just exhausted. I need a break from this world," Smith admitted.

"Maybe you should take a break, let go and be irresponsible for a short period of time," Chanel explained.

"I think I can do that," Smith replied and stretched out on the sofa.

"I have just the thing for you. Get on the floor," Chanel said. There was a puzzled look on Smith's face.

"Trust me," Chanel said.

As Smith sat on the carpet, Chanel pulled her shirt off.

"Why do I think that you are taking advantage of a vulnerable woman right now?" Smith questioned.

"Maybe I am," Chanel answered while she grabbed a bottle of baby oil from the table. She then took her bra off and told Smith to lay on her stomach. As Chanel poured a handful of baby oil onto Smith's soft skin she tensed up.

"Wow, you need a massage bad," Chanel said as she massaged Smith's shoulders while reducing the tension in her body.

"That feels so good," Smith said with a quiet voice. Chanel dug her fingers into Smith's back and slid her hands around the edges of her breasts. Chanel then mounted Smith's back and dug deeper with her elbows while kissing the back of her neck. Smith then rolled onto her back and pulled Chanel's face to hers. Their tongues locked together, tasting their salvia and the emotional juices that leaked from her breasts. Chanel removed Smith's shirt and bra, allowing the two naked bodies to press against each other.

Chanel seemed to kiss every part of Smith's body while removing her shorts and panties. Smith's back arched as the sensation from the tongue and fingers parting her vaginal lips drove her insane. While Smith felt like she was about to explode, the slightest touch around her womb would have taken her there.

"Oh, right there." Smith vocalized her pleasure. Chanel loved pleasing her while pulling all control from her hands. Smith grabbed a handful of Chanel's hair and shoved her face deep into her womb.

"I'm about to come... I'm coming." Smith's moans encouraged Chanel to please her more.

"Shit... I'm coming!" Smith yelled as her body went into convulsions. Chanel licked her lips and wiped the juices from her mouth. Smith sat up and kissed Chanel's lips, pushing her down on her back to gain access to her throbbing vagina. Smith spread Chanel's legs and licked her clitoris in slow circles as she fingered her simultaneously. Chanel rested on her elbows as she watched Smith feast on her womb. There was a look in her eyes that turned Chanel on. She began grinding her hips against Smith's face in circular motions.

"Fuck!" Chanel mumbled. She tried to fight back the urge of exploding but it was inevitable. Chanel came in Smith's mouth as Smith tasted the juices. They moved in between each other's legs and grinded their juice-soaked womb against each other. Smith bit down on her lip as the sensation set her on fire. Chanel pinched Smith's nipples, enjoying the chemistry between the two of them.

Smith got up and went into the bedroom and returned with a vibrator and a nine-inch dildo.

"I knew you were a freak," Chanel teased as Smith returned with the sex toys and lubricant.

"My husband wasn't cutting it, so I went shopping," Smith said as she rubbed the dildo on the side of Chanel's face. She then put it in Chanel's mouth and watched as she devoured every inch. Chanel then spit it out and spread her legs apart. Smith fed the dildo into her snatch and stroked her with long strides. While she was fucking Chanel with the dildo, Smith stuck the vibrator in her ass causing Chanel to nearly bolt from the floor. Smith had completely flipped the switch and became the dominant one. Chanel then took the dildo from Smith's hand and turned Smith over on all fours. She spit into her ass and slowly shoved the head of the dildo inside of her. Smith gripped the carpet so tight she nearly pulled it from the floor. Smith's body was tense, but once the dildo was fully inserted, she relaxed and enjoyed the ride. Chanel then placed it in her vagina and turned it all the way up. Chanel pinned her down and fucked her until Smith exploded like an active volcano. By now, the two of them were exhausted. Smith decided to bath in the juices as she quickly fell asleep. Chanel showered and fell asleep along Smith's side.

* * *

The world was filled with a variety of mysteries and untold tales of days gone by. Most people never saw the colorful adventures of life; the cycle of being intrigued by the multi-cultural differences in society. It was all so alluring and captivating. No one saw past the deceit, the distractions that hid the darkness in plain sight. To be honest, we all missed seeing the obscure until it was hovering over our heads like a morning fog. By then, it was too late.

*   *   *

They sat in the rowboat and gazed into the dark sky, observing the endless number of stars and the beauty of the Milky Way. Tianna loved the intricacies of the celestial bodies that illuminated the darkness. She closed her eyes and took a long pull from a cigar filled with Marijuana. Tianna and her best friend oftentimes came out onto the river late at night to smoke weed and watch the stars. Tianna wasn't as radical and rebellious as her friend; preferring to be more reserved.

"What do you think will happen to us in the future?"

"I don't know. Maybe we'll become movie stars or end up being wives and mothers with too many kids to corral," Tianna joked.

Jasmine Winters was Tianna's best friend. She was given that name when the two of them ran away from the Child Care Center in Chicago during the dead of winter.

"Fuck that. I'm not going to be no damn house-sitting, baby-watching, ass-wife," Winters stated. She took a deep pull from her cigar and blew smoke into the air. "I'm going to be a professional dancer," she added with a beam of expectation in her eyes.

Tianna wanted to do something with her life and take advantage of her youth. She didn't want to wake up one morning in her thirties and be disadvantaged, broke, and struggling to survive.

Tianna and Winters headed back to land. Once they reached the tree line and started the short walk back to the group home, Winters stopped and grabbed hold of Tianna's hair.

"I want you to promise me one thing."

"What's that?" Tianna asked.

"The river, if something was to ever happen to me, that's where I want to be."

"Why are you talking as if you are going to die?" Tianna asked.

"Just promise me," Winters insisted.

"Okay, I promise," Tianna assured her and never asked another question. She and Winters were closer than any two people in this world. Winters just seemed disturbed. She had an old soul and her outlook on things was always nonchalant. Tianna loved her nonetheless and vowed to be there no matter what.

CHAPTER TWENTY-NINE

Victoria

Trust can be a mother fucker, a real pain in the ass. We never knew who was extending their gift of trust. Most of the time it's blindly discarded without a single thought or concern. The ironic thing is the fact that we don't expect to be betrayed or disappointed.

Victoria smiled as Jasmine got inside the car. She was beaming with joy and couldn't stop smiling. "Guess what?" Jasmine announced.

"What?" Victoria answered.

"I get another audition for the leading role."

"I'm so happy for you." Victoria joined her in their excitement while they smiled in unison.

"So what now?" Victoria added.

"They will forward a part of the main character's dialogue and ask me to read lines in front of the directors." Jasmine explained.

"What is this play about?" Victoria asked.

"It's about a girl who was too privileged for her own good. Her mother shielded her from the ugliness of the world, leaving the young girl all alone. The girl developed a mental illness which was never noticed. This girl created imaginary friends in her head to play with and create bonds. She was so lonely and in the need of friends that she thought the imaginary people were real. She even fell in love with one of them, and before she could be saved, tragedy struck. The girl eventually discovers the truth that these friends of hers were created within the confines of her mind. She died as her world came crashing down," Jasmine explained.

"Sounds fascinating," Victoria replied. "Let's go out and celebrate your success."

"Why the hell not," Jasmine replied.

The girls decided to dine at a simple sea food restaurant. Nothing upscale and over the top. Jasmine was a simple person and didn't care much for the illustrious lifestyle.

"I'm excited for you. I truly am," Victoria voiced her support.

"I'm just happy that I have the opportunity to showcase my talent," Jasmine responded.

"The music seems so sad," Victoria said,

"The Ballet is a passionate art as is the contemporary dance. But this play is a mixture of both," Jasmine explained.

While Victoria was listening to Jasmine talk, her mind shifted to another time and place she had not revisited in some time.

"Are you scared?" The girl asked Victoria. "You're shaking," she added.

Victoria had the dream many times before when sleeping was a nightly struggle. But one day the dream suddenly stopped and morphed into a distant memory. Victoria knew the dream well; perhaps something that actually happened. While the girl in the dream was someone she felt connected to, she couldn't recall her face, nor remember the girl's name.

Victoria was afraid, even petrified. She watched the currents generate the flow of the river as it crashed into the riverbank. Victoria told the girl that she was not scared and that she was fine. The two of them faced each other and locked eyes. She felt the hand of a sudden stranger rise to her chin and kiss her lips.

"Do you love me?" she questioned.

"Of course I love you." Victoria had no idea where these words came from, but she knew they were real. Her heart told her so. "Why would you ask if I loved you?"

"Because I need to know," the woman replied. She knew I loved her, that was obvious. I had no idea why I did not run or bolt at the eerie feeling that turned in my stomach. A lot of things were distorted at this time; foggy and unclear. I didn't recall what transpired after my gut wrenching feeling. Everything, it seemed, fast forwarded to the thing I feared the most. I remember drowning, that burning sensation you experience when your lungs take on too much water, and the struggle to survive.

Victoria's body was pulled further into the abyss and there was nothing she could do. Victoria was at the mercy of the river. As she struggled to breathe and fight her way to the surface, she saw the strange woman smiling as she stood at the edge of the riverbank. The woman watched Victoria die and fade away as the current pulled her down under.

*   *   *

"Hello, are you still here?" Jasmine asked as she waved her hand in Victoria's face.

"I'm sorry. My mind went elsewhere," Victoria replied while blinking her eyes a few times, trying to bring her mind back to the present.

"You must have had some thoughts in that head of yours."

"It was nothing," Victoria lied. She had no idea what the dreamt meant or why it stuck in her head like a mouth full of taffy. The drive back to the house was quiet. It was obvious that Victoria had something on her mind.

A ringing phone awakened Victoria from a deep sleep. She looked at the clock on her nightstand and could see that it was very late and wondered who might call her at this hour.

"Hello," she answered while half asleep.

"You sound like you had one hell of a night," the voice stated.

Victoria recognized Chanel's voice on the phone and knew it was Chanel. "My nights are always eventful. Finding time to sleep is the difficult part. It seems like our timing is never aligned to meet up," Victoria said.

"Time never seems to sit around for no one, but the thing isn't always time. It's opportunity," Chanel explained.

"So why are you calling so early?" Victoria asked.

"Because I saw you in a dream. Now I'm trying to make some sense out of it, and to determine what connects the two of us," Chanel stated.

"Maybe it's just a simple dream and you're looking too deep into it," Victoria replied.

"We overlook a lot of things; miss the silver lining in the gray areas that go unnoticed. Everything is designed for a purpose, even dreams," Chanel explained.

"So what does this have to do with me?" Victoria asked.

"You're one of the stars in the show darling. You just don't know it yet," Chanel stated.

"Someone told me something similar before, and I'm just as confused now as I was then." Victoria said as she stood and walked to the window.

"I saw you the night you came into club BED. You walked past me and got on the elevator." Chanel said.

"I don't recall," Victoria replied.

"Of course you don't, but I was there. I think there's something between the two of us and ever since our encounter back in Canada I've had some strange things happen to me. Things I could never explain," Chanel explained.

"Me too," Victoria admitted.

"Such as?" Chanel pressed for information.

"One incident in particular. On the day that we were to meet, there was this waitress who thought I'd just left, and then came back in different attire and placed the same order. She knew exactly what I wanted and to add to the confusion, there was this bird..."

"A white one with familiar eyes that you felt drawn to. I saw the same bird before and I nearly fell from a window ledge pursuing it," Chanel interrupted. As Chanel spoke of the mysterious bird, Victoria was floored with so much uncertainty. She felt as if she was living a dream. Her mind tried to process any rational thoughts available, but things were just too complicated.

"Does this sound familiar to you?" Chanel asked.

"You can be talking about any bird. I don't think I can truly trust my judgement at this time. There is too much questionable information," Victoria summarized.

"So, how has California been treating you?" Chanel thought it best to change the subject.

"It's been great. I found a guide, someone whose been showing me around. She's quite the character, full of energy and high spirited," Victoria said.

"Sounds like someone I know," Chanel replied.

"I can see the two of you getting along quite well," Victoria commented.

"Maybe so, does this person have a name?"

"Jasmine. Her name is Jasmine," Victoria responded.

Chanel grew quiet, wondering if this could possibly be her Jasmine. The description of her personality matches, but it could be anyone. Chanel knew that Jasmine was toxic and that she had to end their relationship. Although it would be a painful, it was something that had to be done.

"She sounds like quite the person," Chanel said.

"She can be. Enough about her. When can we meet up again?" Victoria inquired, hoping that this time it would actually happen.

"When the time is right," Chanel replied.

"And when should that be?" Victoria asked.

"I don't know. I kind of like the mystery, the somewhat anonymous aspect of being acquainted," Chanel replied.

Victoria wasn't into the games Chanel was trying to play, but what other choice did she have?

"Tell me something. What's your biggest fear in this world?" Chanel asked.

"I'm afraid of drowning," Victoria replied. "Why do you want to know?"

"There's a lot to learn from people by knowing what they fear," Chanel stated.

"So what does that say about me?" Victoria asked.

"It tells me the reason you are afraid of drowning is because you can't swim. So maybe drowning isn't one of your fears after all," Chanel stated.

Chanel made a lot of sense over something so basic and small. "So what are you afraid of?" Victoria challenged Chanel.

"Sobriety. I'm afraid of being sober long enough to face myself. So maybe I should say I'm afraid of myself." Chanel's voice sounded sincere and sad. Victoria felt her emotions stir as she considered what Chanel was going through. The worst kind of prison is the mental one; being condemned and confined to time within the mental compartment of your own thoughts.

"I think we're all on some sort of a journey trying to find ourselves before it's too late," Victoria offered.

"Or we're just broken, and somethings that break can never be fixed," Chanel replied. "What do you see when you look into a mirror?" Chanel questioned.

Victoria couldn't answer immediately. Instead, she closed her eyes and saw Lana in the bed dying. She had no idea why that image flashed in her head.

"I don't see anything," Victoria stated.

"That's because you're not looking. Once you learn to look pass your physical appearance, you'll see more than an image. You'll see everything you need to know," Chanel explained. While she was thinking about what was being conveyed to her Chanel broke her train of thought.

"I have to go but I'll contact you at another time." Chanel ended the call before Victoria had a chance to reply.

CHAPTER THIRTY

Chanel

Chanel believed sobriety to be her mortal enemy and that heroin was a jealous lover; and if it couldn't have you, no one could. Smith stood by her side and offered support as best she could. Being a drug addict was one thing, but total withdrawal drew unimageable pain. For Chanel, dying was an option.

Smith walked into the room holding two cups of hot tea with a touch of honey. The two of them had formed a deep friendship. Smith sat on the bed and rubbed Chanel's side as she curled up into a fetal position, sweating and rocking back and forth hoping to distract some of the pain.

"I have some tea for you," Smith announced.

"If it doesn't have any crack or heroin in it, I'll pass." Smith turned her face and smacked her lips indicating that the tea was very tasty.

"Just joking," Chanel said.

Smith was amazed at Chanel's bravery and audacious ways; the will to persevere and press forward. Chanel had weathered a life of abuse and pain; a true survivor. Chanel turned on her side to face Smith.

"When I was in that coma, I heard you speak every night. I held on to your words. But I can't get this little girl out of my head. It was like I had this out-of-body experience.

I was walking down the halls of the hospital and this little girl called me into her room. Her name was Casey. She was fighting leukemia. She told me that I should go see my friend before it was too late; the girl with the pretty smile like yours in room 321," Chanel explained.

"What do you think it means?" Smith asked.

"I don't know, but it has to mean something. This wasn't a dream or some empty daydream. I mean, I heard everything you said while I was out of it. So, why can't this be true?" Chanel questioned.

Smith grew quiet and brushed the hair from her face. She needed to tell Chanel about Jasmine. It was killing her on the inside.

"Remember when we were in the hospital, the day you woke up and asked if anyone had been to see you?"

"I remember," Chanel answered.

"Well, I wasn't telling the truth. This girl showed up out of the blue and asked if you were dead. Once I told her your condition was unclear, she left. I ran after her, but she was gone. I thought that I was hallucinating. It happened so fast," Smith explained.

"Why would you lie?" Chanel was confused.

"I don't know. I truly felt like I was hallucinating, and I had no idea what to believe. I was tired and emotionally drained," Smith explained.

"Jasmine and I are too much alike and toxic to each other. We've always had each other's back. But if I want to live, I have to let her go," Chanel admitted.

"I don't think running away from your problem would help," Smith added.

"You don't know Jasmine, and problems were not the only thing I'm running from. Me putting some distance between the two of us could save her as well," Chanel explained.

"Life is so complicated." Smith stated.

"As we are intricate," Chanel added. She closed her eyes while her mind returned to that little girl in the hospital.

"So what do you think of her?" Chanel asked.

"Think of who?" Smith questioned.

"Jasmine," Chanel stated.

"Our encounter was brief. I don't know how I could answer that."

"What did you think when you first saw her?" Chanel was curious.

"Besides being startled, I thought she was beautiful," Smith added.

"Jasmine taught me how to love myself and embrace my sexuality. She was the first woman that I'd ever touched, kissed and tasted. Jasmine was my first orgasm and first love. She saved me from being locked in my head, and I never thought I could move on without her," Chanel explained.

"You two sound like you were extremely close," Smith observed.

"That we are."

"You spoke briefly about her in one of your sessions but never in depth. Why is that?"

"Some things I'm just not into sharing, and Jasmine is one of those things," Chanel replied.

"When we were in the shower, I noticed the scar along your spine," Chanel said,

"I was in a bad car accident when I was a child. I was in a coma for a period and had a serious head injury. I lost my memory, broke my back, and fractured my skull. It was quite the experience."

"I think bad experiences make for better stories. Besides, who doesn't like scars with impressionable features?" Chanel rolled back over and began rocking herself. She wanted to embrace the pain, instead of distracting herself from the trauma. While this might not work for others, it worked for her.

*   *   *

"Wake up sleepy head," the little girl said as she shook Chanel. When Chanel saw that it was Casey, she sat up quickly.

"What are you doing here?" Chanel asked while noticing that Casey was no longer bald. She had a head full of long sandy brown hair, and her piercing blue eyes were beaming with curiosity.

"There's a very sick man in the other room. Let's go see him." Casey grabbed Chanel's hand. The old house looked familiar. Chanel was trying to process what was transpiring. Casey led the way. They came upon an old door. Casey turned the knob and pushed it open.

"We have to be really quiet and not wake him, because he will get mad," Casey whispered. When they creep into the room, and Chanel saw who the man was, she covered her mouth to keep from screaming. Her eyes watered as she felt a lump develop in her throat. It was Jeffrey Smith, the man that Chanel called her father, and the man who raped her. He was dying and his body was fragile and weak. He could be heard gasping for air as he struggled to breathe.

"He's going to die," Casey said. Chanel closed her eyes thinking that this had to be a dream. Casey told her to say goodbye to Jeffrey as Chanel shook her head no. When Chanel opened her eyes and stared at Casey, those big crystal blue eyes had turned black and demonic. Chanel ran out of the room and down the hallway. When she finally turned the corner, there was a door leading to her childhood bedroom, the one place where she always felt safe. Chanel slowly opened the door and entered the room. She saw a little girl curled up in the corner.

"It's okay to come out," Chanel said and waved for the girl.

"He told me not to leave the closet or I would get into trouble," the little girl said.

"There's no one here. You're safe," Chanel replied. When the little girl looked up, she looked familiar. It then hit her. It was Smith. Chanel screamed to the top of her lungs and shook her head while covering her ears.

"Chanel, wakeup. Wakeup." Smith shook her from the nightmare as Chanel bolted from her sleep, panting and out of breath.

"It was that little girl again. Then I saw her father and then I saw you. Just a younger version," Chanel explained as Smith held her like a little child and told her it was only a dream. Smith knew Chanel had a lot of things to deal with and now that she was sober, they would only get worse.

CHAPTER THRITY-ONE

Victoria

The night was young, and Victoria was content. She sat near the water and drank from a glass of wine. Jasmine was away practicing for her final audition, leaving Victoria all to herself. It's amazing what idle time does for the human psyche. Victoria bathed in the pleasures of her recently acquired awareness that provided a sense of purpose. Things were different now; the air seemed lighter and the weight on her shoulders had been lifted.

While the world was vast in its nature, it lacked emotional energy. Some people were sad and angry no matter what part of the planet they occupied, but others were happy, excited, and even anxious. Emotions — good or bad — tied the world together much like a universal language spoken by every living thing. Victoria's thoughts shifted from unpretentious to inveigling and salacious.

Cheri popped into Victoria's head like a flashing thought of the day. Cheri was the young woman that Victoria had met on the dance floor of Club BED; the first woman that sexually aroused Victoria in an unimagined way. As Victoria continued sipping her wine, she felt her breathing increase as memories of Cheri were recalled. Victoria remembered Cheri kissing her neck while reaching under her dress and pulling her silk panties aside. Cheri's fingers parting her vaginal lips and the sensations that ensued; and even the redolence of the bathroom stall.

Victoria still remembered the taste of Cheri's tongue, the texture of her lips, and what she smelled like. Her wetness increased as each passing second fed additional recollections of what happened that night; putting her legs on Cheri's shoulders while she devoured her sweetness; and the licking and pinching of her nipples. The mere thoughts of the night consumed Victoria.

Victoria finished the glass of wine and moved to the bottle. While laying on her back, she rubbed herself, allowing the moment to take her back into the bathroom stall where the encounter began. Slight moans were followed by the juices overflowing with nectar. Victoria lost all her inhibitions and removed her panties. Victoria spread her legs and slowly inserted the neck of the wine bottle inside her vagina. The bottle slid in and out as she arched her back and pushed deeper. The neck of the bottle was shiny from the thick white juices that covered it. Victoria came as she stroked herself at a faster pace. A second, even more satisfying orgasm came forth. Victoria's body relaxed as the memories began to subside.

While Victoria looked for clarity, she remembered going to Club BED and seeing a girl cleaning-up a spillage near the back entrance. Victoria recalled getting on the elevator, and in a brief instance, she and the girl locked eyes. There she was — it was Chanel.

* * *

"This place has your name written all over it," Jason said the moment he walked into Victoria's new home. He and Valerie had just flown into the states and had business dealings that concerned Bloom Capital. Victoria had plans to open an office in the U.S., and now it was about to happen.

"It's just something temporary. I have another place being built," Victoria explained.

Valerie smiled as she took a seat next to Victoria on the sofa.

"So, what's the plan?" Victoria inquired.

"Well, once we take care of the kinks, and iron out all of the paperwork, Valerie will take it from there." Jason explained.

Victoria turned her attention to Valerie. "I've scouted a few spaces and have narrowed the search down to two locations. Once I've completed that task, I'm open to receiving resumes and interviewing people to fill the positions," Victoria explained.

"How much time?" Victoria added.

"Six to eight months, give or take," Valerie answered.

"Numbers." Victoria wanted all of the details.

"We're on the plus side of the market. As of now, there's a twelve percent increase per quarter. The big project we have now is actually here in California," Valerie explained.

"Which is?"

"A production company called Wave. We're financing a family project," Jason explained which drew Victoria's attention.

"Where's the portfolio on this?" Victoria asked. Valerie went through her things and retrieved the file. Once Victoria opened it, her mind processed the information with absolute intrigue. As she read more into it, some of the names behind the company stood out. Victoria knew a few of the executive producers from past events she'd attended. This was something she wanted to study.

"Leave this file with me," Victoria said while putting the file away.

"The realtor will place Lana's house on the market. I'll be sure to keep you in the loop," Valerie added. Victoria wanted nothing to do with her childhood home and selling it was the best thing to do.

"So you're really going through with this?" Jason asked.

"I have to," Victoria replied and he understood. There was no telling what the future held for Victoria, and such uncertainty left Jason unsettled. He loved Victoria, but deep down he knew Victoria was unable to reciprocate.

Dreams are like windows, providing us with the opportunity to study our past and peer into the future. Images provide the space and time to digest their true meaning. Sometimes we find our reflection a bit unfamiliar, until the small gestures appear, reminding us of who we are. We don't have the option to reinvent our circumstances. It's by luck, or possibly by chance

*that we're dealt a decent hand before sitting at the table. While
sometimes unclear, we're all connected to a similar fate. While
some find a way to unbind themselves from such kismet, it still
finds a way to pull us back into this life or the next.*

Victoria was experiencing the worst day of her life, and there was
no indication that peace could be found. She'd just buried her mother
and the sight of Lana's lifeless body was traumatizing. Seeing her with
a forced smile, and flushed cheeks was heart breaking. Victoria hoped
her mother would wake up and admit that this was all a silly prank.
Victoria had cried all she could cry, and there was nothing left for her
to do but heal.

Victoria walked into Lana's bedroom and looked around, not really
sure what she was in search of. Her mother took pride in being self-
sufficient, and that led to her obsession of materialistically enriching
herself with possessions. Lana had a plethora of things from clothing to
jewelry and other accessories worth millions of dollars. She walked into
the massive closet and looked at the clothes and shoe boxes. Victoria ran
her hand through the row of dresses and sat on the floor. There was a
bunch of boxes on the floor next to her. She opened the first one and
found a pair of fire-red Prada heels which were not Lana's style. Then
Victoria opened a second box and found a pair of Alexander McQueen
pumps. This was Lana for sure. Victoria smiled and put the pumps
back into the box.

While putting the box away, something caught her attention.
Victoria climbed the step-ladder in front of her and pulled a small
lock-box from one of the shelves. She sat back down on the floor and
opened the lock-box that contained several old photographs taken years
ago. Victoria smiled as she flipped through the photos. She returned
the photos to the box and found an envelope full of papers. On top of
the papers was a folder labeled **Adoption Agency.**

Her eyes questioned her brain as it broke down what was in the papers.
While totally confused and an emotional wreck, Victoria questioned
whether the papers were correct. According to the documents, Victoria
was adopted. How could that be possible? Victoria thought. Why would

Lana keep this from her? Victoria was trying to deal with Lana's death and now this.

Once Victoria finished reading the documents, her mind drew nothing but blanks. She closed her eyes for a moment and tried to think of something more soothing, but nothing emerged. She vowed to find some answers to determine if the adoption was real. Victoria had never doubted anything that Lana had told her. But for now, Victoria wondered if her entire life was a lie.

CHAPTER THIRTY-TWO

Jasmine

Dancing kept me grounded; liberated me; gave me a sense of freedom; and made me feel as if there wasn't a care in the world. Swaying my hips was both sensual and intimate. I was in tune with every inch of my body.

Without dancing, I had nothing. My life was stuck in a constant cycle of chaos and organized pandemonium. Although I tried not to focus on the blurred lines that penciled in the gray areas, they stood out. Life has a way of making you pay attention, especially to the disadvantages you're forced to endure.

Dancing gave me the control I needed to move on; allowing my body to move in sync with the music. I graced the notes in each chord orchestrated by a divine symphonist. I was a mere bird allowing the wind under my wings to carry me.

It was ironic how life provided so many escapes and then snatched them away without a warning. I took advantage of the moment and embraced reality for what it was.

Jasmine took to the stage and embraced the sound of water rushing down the canal. Her white attire reflected an angelic glow as she danced; swaying her hips and holding her arms out to be guided by an invisible force. She levitated her energy beyond that of humanly consuetude, thrusting her body forward while making use of the entire stage. Her mixture of ballet and contemporary dance was pleasing to the eye.

Another dancer appeared from the shadows of the stage. Their synchronized movements complimented the choreography and revealed their passion. As the music intensified, they held each other while their bodies merged into one. The second dancer stared into Jasmine's eyes, held her waist, and shared the aura that lifted her into the spiritual realms.

Other dancers soon joined them on the stage. The story of a fallen angel being casted from heaven was told as their bodies moved in unison, articulating themselves in the absence of words while speaking in the language of body movements and vibrations.

The house lights came on indicating the end of the show. Applause warranted three encores from the cast signifying a *"job well done."* The dancers left the stage while the crowd shared their appreciation for such a brilliant piece of art.

The girl who danced with Jasmine in the duet was mesmerizing. Aside from her true beauty, she was a great dancer; exceptional even. As she gathered herself and left the stage, she walked past Jasmine and didn't introduce herself. By this time, Jasmine was in the shower with a few of the other dancers. While she was under the water washing her hair, she looked up and saw the girl who accompanied her in the duet. Although the two of them danced together like life-long partners, this was their first time together. In case of a no-show, all of the dancers had to know the choreography. That was the case tonight.

"Hi, I'm Jasmine."

"I'm Amber, nice to meet you," she replied in a heavy British accent. Amber was beautiful and Jasmine couldn't stop staring at her. Amber's teeth were pearl-white; long, natural red hair; and thin crisp lips that appeared both edible and tempting. Jasmine could not stop gawking at Amber's beauty.

"I'm sorry," Jasmine said with a slight chuckle.

"For what?" Amber asked.

"For staring. You're really beautiful, like you should have been a model."

"Bad feet, I'm a dancer." Amber responded with a smile.

"So, where are you from?" Amber asked.

"Originally, I'm from the United Kingdom, Liverpool. But I moved to the United States when I was nineteen to attend the Ballet Academy of Dance in New York," Jasmine explained. "You're a great dancer," Jasmine added.

"Like wise," Amber replied while stepping out of the shower. As she wrapped the towel around her body, Jasmine approached.

"I don't want to sound like I'm a weirdo, but would you like to have lunch with me?" Jasmine asked.

Amber's artic, blue eyes squinted with a curious gaze. "I don't do lunch," she replied. There was a look of defeat in Jasmine's eyes. "Dinner, we can do dinner," Amber added as she walked away with a smile. Jasmine smiled back and took a seat on the bench. While Jasmine had no idea what had drawn her to Amber, she was about to find out.

The next day Jasmine and Amber met at Amber's apartment, but the last thing on their mind was dinner. Jasmine entered Amber's apartment, and even without a hello, Amber was all over Jasmine. They began kissing and licking each other as if lust was seeping from their pores. Amber palmed Jasmine's ass while lifting up her dress.

"You smell so good," Amber said. This was a side of Amber that took Jasmine by surprise. She was more aggressive and eager to indulge, to unfold herself as if she had layers of forbidden skin. She was exposed and bare, offering herself in ways that only the privileged could access. As Amber's robe came undone, her pierced nipples and vagina sparked Jasmine's desires. Her mouth watered with anticipation, and her heart pounded hard and fast. Amber was sucking on Jasmine's neck, biting her ear and fondling her breast.

"You look surprised," Amber said as she stopped to take a breath.

"That's because I am."

"Take this off." Amber instructed and pulled Jasmine's dress over her shoulders, undid her bra, and pulled off her panties. Jasmine's succulent breast enticed Amber to devour them individually. Their arousal grew quickly, filling the room with the scent of their natural juices.

Amber took hold of Jasmine's hand and led her to the bedroom. While Amber advised Jasmine to get comfortable, she headed to the closet. She returned with a red box that sparked Jasmine's curiosity. Amber opened the box and removed a massive fourteen-inch dildo, a vibrator and a bottle of oil. She approached Jasmine and had her lay out on the bed. She poured oil over her body and massaged it deep into her flesh.

As Jasmine bit down on her bottom lip, Amber's hand slid into the crease of her inner thigh causing Jasmine to squirm. Amber opened both her legs with ease. The heat from her vagina could be felt against her flesh. Amber licked her inner thighs and headed straight for the main course. Jasmine's mound was bald, pink and wet.

Amber was by far the most beautiful woman Jasmine had ever seen. The acts being played out felt like a dream that Jasmine refused to leave. Amber kissed her vaginal lips and climbed her body. Her piercing blue eyes locked onto Jasmine's soul.

As they embraced, the friction from their bare skin ignited an emotional flame. Jasmine parted Amber's vaginal lips with three fingers, wrapped her legs around Amber's waist and dug into her back. She then headed back to her snatch, and this time, she tasted her. Amber focused on Jasmine's clitoris and licked it with a stiff tongue, spreading her pussy and sucking her flesh with her mouth.

Amber reached for the high-speed vibrator and slowly penetrated Jasmine's anal cavity. It took her by surprise and she nearly bolted from the bed. Her quiet moans went from docile to partial screams. Amber drove her to the point of sexual bliss. Jasmine's ululation turned her on, causing Amber to want her more. As Amber stroked her anal cavity with the vibrator, she simultaneously ate her womb. The vibrations beneath Amber's body was an indication that she was on the verge of coming. Jasmine opened her legs and locked them behind her head. While Amber had full access to her snatch, she ate her with sloppy manners. The vibrator was on high speed probing in and out of her ass. Jasmine exploded violently and rolled away from her grasp.

"Fuck! What you trying to give me a heart attack?" Jasmine questioned as she brushed the hair from her face.

"If you allow me." Amber replied and pulled her back onto the bed and went back to pleasing her. When she pulled the massive dildo out, Jasmine told her to wait.

"I've never had anything remotely close to that, so you have to take your time with that thing," Jasmine explained.

"I got you baby." Amber assured her and spit on the rubber head of the monstrous toy. The huge mushroom shaped head slowly opened her up and Jasmine tensed up. By the fourth inch, she was gripping the satin sheets so tight her knuckles turned a pale white.

"Shit!" Jasmine moaned in a mixture of pain and pleasure. Once her womb took all of its girth and length, she relaxed a bit, and allowed herself to be pleasured. Amber stroked her slowly while massaging her pussy at the same time. As she increased the pace and pounded her at a much quicker speed, Jasmine started to run but couldn't escape Amber's grasp. The giant penis killed her insides and brought on an immediate orgasm. Jasmine's thick, white juices coated the rubber shaft like a second layer of skin. Jasmine came more times that she could remember. Now it was Amber's turn.

She made Amber get on all fours and beg to be fucked. When she positioned the dildo near her vagina, Amber lowered her body so the head on the giant monster was near her anal cavity. Jasmine was a bit apprehensive about penetrating her small hole with such a huge penis. Amber reached underneath herself and held it steady, slowly easing onto the dildo until it was fully consumed.

Jasmine was impressed by Amber's sexual ability to take so much dick without flinching an inch. Although Amber wasn't much of a screamer, her moans were light and sensual. But it was written all over her face that she was being satisfied.

Amber reached for the vibrator and shoved it in and out of her snatch. "Fuck me harder, please?" Amber asked with a wrinkled expression. While Jasmine pounded her hole, she backed herself up into each stroke, challenging her sexual advances. Amber's pussy came and squirted over the vibrator as she rocked from side to side feeling the orgasmic wave rattle her body.

The two of them took turns pleasing each other until they became exhausted. Jasmine had never experienced such intensity that drained her of all the energy in her body.

I'm driven by desires that pursue my soul,
like a lover's vengeance.
Call my name in whispers
that could be heard for miles.
Sexually aroused, conquered hands
touched me with ease.
Stifled by lust,
pleased with your eyes that touch my soul.
Invading my divinity with intimacy
that hugs my vulnerabilities.
Needing to feel you inside me, beside me,
despise me like broken dreams.
Drown me in your desires
and free my mind from all restraints,
I admire your advances.
Longing to taste your lips,
feel you deep inside my folds.
As I, As I,
remember your embrace
and unite our souls.

* * *

There was something peaceful and calm about the mornings; perhaps my favorite time of the day. I couldn't sense whether today would be productive or contain an onslaught of chaotic energy. Either way, life still had to go on.

"You're still here?" Amber asked as she approached Jasmine near the window with a blanket wrapped around her naked body. "I was sure you would have taken off like a thief in the night." Amber added. Jasmine met her gaze, still mesmerized by her beauty.

Jasmine smiled and took a pull from the cigarette and blew the smoke into the air as she turned towards Amber. "Normally I would have been in the wind, but we're in the same dance company, plus I'm not really done with you yet." Jasmine leaned forward. "I'm still intrigued by you," Jasmine said as she kissed her lips.

Amber took the cigarette from her hand. "So, what's your story?"

"Nothing worth telling," Jasmine answered.

"I'm sure there's something there. You just have to open up and let me in that head of yours." Amber stated.

"Why, you trying to save me?"

"Who said anything about saving? We have ways of expressing ourselves without speaking a single word. When you dance, I see you. I see your pain in the way you move your hips. Your posture tells me you're running from something," Amber explained.

"Dancing is like finding yourself after losing touch with who you are. It's an escape for me and a place I run to hide from the ugly side of the world. I know it's not the answer to my problems, but if only for a short time, I'd take it over anything in the world," Jasmine replied.

"Nothing in life is simple, but that's the beauty in it. We get to put our strengths on full display. I know you'll find your way in due time," Amber responded.

"Let's hope you're right."

"And wish you're wrong," Amber said. "I'm sure I'm not the only girl you're interested in. So, who's the other smile on the other side of the pillow?"

"I don't do relationships. I'm bad at love. But I do have a best friend, and we have a relationship that's hard to explain. We're sisters, lover's, besties, everything to each other. But for me, a lot of it is hard to take," Jasmine explained.

"Why is that?" Amber asked with a curious expression on her face.

"She's sick, not physically, but mentally. She has these imaginary people in her head that she believes to be real. I play along with her illness because it's what keeps her going. Besides, isn't that what best friends are for?" Jasmine explained.

The look in her eyes was sincere and tied to a bond that could not be broken. A tear broke free and ran down her cheek. While Amber felt the sadness that surfaced from her aura, she didn't have any words to console her. She touched Jasmine's thigh and left her in thought.

* * *

Jasmine found Amber sleeping on the sofa and was careful not to wake her. She wrote a note for her and stuck it under the bedroom door. She liked Amber and thought that they could become friends. She brushed a strand of hair from her forehead and left the apartment. When she made it to her car, she pulled her cell out and called Victoria. As of lately, the two of them had not spent much time together. But Victoria didn't read too much into her absence since Jasmine was busy with dance auditions. After a few rings she picked up the phone.

"Hi, did I wake you?" Jasmine asked.

"No, I was up. How have you been?" Victoria inquired.

"Busy, but I'll manage. I've been pouring myself into the dance auditions. We're pretty sure that all of the people in the company are in the play," Jasmine replied.

"I'm excited for you. I think you'll find yourself in the position you've always wanted," Victoria said.

"I hope so."

"Just always be honest, no matter how brutal it might seem," Victoria said. There was a silence on the other end of the phone, one that went on too long.

"Hello, are you still. there?" Victoria asked.

"Yeah, I was just thinking."

"You seem a bit out of it. Are you alright?" Victoria was concerned. Something had Jasmine's attention and it was pulling her energy down. She didn't sound like herself.

"Yeah." She replied unconvincingly. "I'm just searching for something that makes sense," Jasmine added.

"You sure you're alright?" Victoria questioned her again.

"Remember when you told me about those adoption papers you found in your mother's closet? What happen when you began to look into it?" Jasmine asked.

"I chose not to invest my energy into it because it doesn't matter anymore. Lana's my mother," Victoria explained.

"Don't you want to find out where you came from and who your real family is?" Jasmine asked. She could sense that Victoria was uncomfortable answering these questions.

"Aren't you tired of playing these mind games?" Jasmine asked before her previous question could be answered.

"What games?" Victoria shot back.

"I think you should get some help. This has been going on long enough and it's not all your fault because I've helped you dig yourself into a deeper sickness," Jasmine stated.

"I have no idea what you're talking about. But these bullshit riddles you constantly throw in my direction tells me that you're the one who needs help," Victoria snapped. She could hear laughter on the other side of the phone.

"You're so far gone you don't even see how messed up you are. When you wanted to see Chanel did you actually see her?" Jasmine's question caught Victoria off guard. Mainly because Victoria had never told her Chanel's name, let alone the fact that the two of them had made arrangements to meet up. So, the question was, how did she know about Chanel?

"How did you know about Chanel. Are you following me?" That was the only logical question that registered with any kind of rational thought.

"You still don't get it do you?" Jasmine asked while wondering how screwed up Victoria's head was. "I know you have to remember something," Jasmine added.

"You don't know a thing about me, and I have no idea what kind of angle you're working, but I don't want any part of it," Victoria spoke in anger.

"Look between your toes and you'll see something that should jog your memory. You and Chanel, all of you are the same." Jasmine stated.

Jasmine looked at her phone and the battery was dead. Victoria couldn't figure it out even though she was the key to the mystery. Jasmine knew her darkest secrets.

"Shit!" Jasmine vented as she tossed her phone onto the passenger seat.

CHAPTER THIRTY-THREE

Smith

Smith was emotionally drained. Things at home had deteriorated, her husband wanted a divorce, and her life was in a state of confusion. She had lost control and questioned her mental stability.

Smith stepped from her car and climbed the stairs to Kathy Clark's home. This was Smith's breaking point that allowed her to remove all barriers and pursue answers through the guidance of her former mentor and psychiatrist, Dr. Kathy Clark.

"Am I still welcome here?" Smith asked the minute Kathy opened the door.

"Of course you are. Don't be condescending." Kathy welcomed her with opened arms.

As the two of them became comfortable, Smith sensed that her world would become worse after this conversation.

"You seem a bit apprehensive like there's some reluctance for this visit?" Kathy spoke direct.

"I'm just unsure of a lot of things at this point in my life. I thought I had everything under control, but obviously I don't."

"I've known you a long time, and I can see the strides you've taken to make it this far. But you've lost your way," Kathy explained.

"I don't understand."

"I can show you if you like?" Kathy responded.

"How would you do that?" Smith asked.

"Metaphysically, I can put you under hypnosis and show you the things you don't remember."

"I have nothing to lose, why not?" Smith said while she removed her jacket.

"How do we begin?" Smith asked

"Follow me." Kathy led her into a room with an angelic decor, a recliner, and the soothing sound of a small water fountain. Smith was asked to get comfortable and close her eyes.

"I want you to listen to the sound of my voice, and think back to a time you remember, the time when we first visited your broken reality," Kathy instructed. Kathy was burning something that floated through Smith's nostrils and into her lungs. In an instant Smith felt overwhelmed.

"Think about the broken realities," Kathy repeated.

Smith couldn't take the thick smoke that filled her lungs and decided she couldn't continue. She jumped up and saw that she was no longer in the recliner. She wasn't in Kathy's house. She saw a door and opened it. She was in a hospital. She walked down a dimly-lit hallway and came upon a door leading into room 321. Smith slowly opened the door and entered the room. As she walked past the wall, there was the little girl with leukemia. Her name was Casey.

"You're back," Casey said.

"I am," Smith replied while she sat on the edge of the bed. "But I don't know why," Smith admitted.

"That's okay, because I forget things too. My momma says that I'll get better and be able to remember everything in the whole, wide world," Casey said.

"Why did I come back to you?" Smith asked.

"Because one of us had to live and somebody had to die," Casey replied.

"Who had to die," Smith questioned.

"I died so you could live. The Black River. You can't remember because you're sick too," the girl explained.

"How did you die?" Smith asked.

"I drowned in the Black River. But you didn't know I would. None of us did," Casey explained.

"You're just a kid, it's impossible," Smith commented.

"That's because I died a long time ago," Casey commented while her voice began to fade. The walls were collapsing while Smith felt a rush of wind blowing from her room. Smith had no idea what was going on, and before she knew it, she bolted from the hypnosis. Images flashed through her head; a rowboat and a small girl sitting across from her. The girl was in pain and begged for it to end. Smith saw the younger version of herself, trying to reassure Casey that everything would be alright. That was all that she could remember as the tears rolled down her face and her eyes waited to hear a menacing tale.

Kathy saw that Smith had no idea what to make of the newly acquired information. "The two of you were 10 years old when it happened," Kathy explained. "Casey could not swim and neither could her mother who dove into the water from the riverbank and tried to save Casey. But it was too late. They both died that day and you were taken into custody. The state didn't prosecute you because you were deemed unfit to stand trial. So, you were admitted into a mental institution and granted relief when you turned 18. I was your psychiatrist."

"But I'm a psychologist. I can't be a patient," Smith stated.

"I'm afraid that you're not," Kathy answered. "You stopped medicating against the order prescribed to you. You suffer from a condition known as S.D.D. — Social Depression Disorder. It causes your brain to take on chemicals which cause an imbalance. You create imaginary people in your head; people with entire backgrounds, occupations, fears, addictions. You create a void in your head and fill it with people. You jump in and out of these voids with no idea you're doing so. Like Tianna Smith, the psychologist with a husband named Mark. They later divorced and she became involved with a woman," Kathy explained.

Smith stood up and nearly fell when her hand missed the doorknob. "You're lying," Smith yelled.

"I'm afraid that I'm not," Kathy replied. "You can look for yourself. Research the drowning of a mother and a daughter. They called it the

Black River tragedy after their bodies were recovered. You told the investigators that you tried to cure your sister who was your twin. Casey had leukemia and wanted to make it go away. You told the investigators that the river was magical, and that's why you did it," Kathy explained.

"You're a fucking lying bitch!" Smith screamed and stormed out of the room, never to return again.

CHAPTER THIRTY-FOUR

Victoria

Victoria stepped from the shower and wrapped herself in a towel. She sat on the edge of the tub and thought about her argument with Jasmine. The constant riddles and confusing conversations beat-down Victoria's patience, leaving no reason for the maniacal assertions she alleged. Jasmine told Victoria, "look between your toes," as if that made any sense. To satisfy her curiosity, Victoria looked and discovered small puncture marks between her toes, possibly caused by syringes.

Determined to find answers, Victoria got dressed and searched throughout her house for drug related items that required the use of a syringe. Victoria's stress level increased into a near panic state, leaving her on the verge of passing out. She took a seat next to the dresser and talked herself into lowering her anxiety.

She closed her eyes and steadied her breathing — in out, in out, in out, deep breaths. Once she regained her composure, she continued the search. An hour passed and she found nothing. Victoria went into the closet and searched every box, drawer, and handbag. Again, nothing.

Victoria was about to leave the closet when she had a recollection, one she'd never recalled before. For some reason, the medicine cabinet in the bathroom grabbed her attention. She walked into the bathroom and slowly approached the medicine cabinet; preparing for something gruesome and possibly dangerous. Before opening the cabinet, her mind questioned whether she should pursue this path. She then opened the medicine cabinet.

Except for the standard items in a medicine cabinet, there was nothing there. As Victoria continued looking in the cabinet, something stood out. She removed everything, including the glass shelves. She felt along the back wall of the cabinet and discovered a hollow compartment. When Victoria pushed on it, the wall clicked and opened. Inside was a small black pouch. Victoria removed the bag and sat on the edge of the tub. She opened it and found a spoon, lighter, and some used syringes. There were even old baggies with what appeared to be some kind of powder substance inside. Victoria had never used drugs before and was in a state of disbelief. While trying to make sense of what she had seen, the phone rang.

"Hello?" Victoria slowly answered.

"Why do you sound so creepy right now?" Jason asked.

"I'm sorry. I just have a lot on my mind."

"Care to talk about it," Jason asked.

"It's nothing like that," Victoria lied.

"Well, things are going great. Let me tell you this Valerie of yours is a great asset to the company. She is a real work horse." As Jason talked, Victoria's mind was elsewhere.

"Jason, how long have you known me?" Victoria questioned.

"Really? I've known you since we were about 10 years old. Why do you asked?"

"Where did we grow up?" Victoria asked.

"Yellow Knife. What's going on." Jason was puzzled by the direction of this conversation.

"Just trying to fill in some blanks. Have I ever done drugs?" she blurted out.

"I don't know where you're going with this but..."

"Just answer the fucking question, Jason." Victoria snapped.

"You don't remember Winters?"

"No, who is Winters?" Victoria asked.

"The girl who nearly killed you. The two of you were inseparable and were always running away together," Jason explained.

"Running away. From where?" Victoria was becoming even more confused.

"Yellow Knife." Jason replied.

"What happened to her?" Victoria asked.

"After things went bad. You know, her nearly killing you with those drugs, she ran away. I never heard from her again. You were adopted and..."

"Adopted? So you knew Lana wasn't my biological mother?" Victoria questioned.

"Victoria, have you been taking your pills?" Jason asked with a concerned voice.

"Of course," Victoria lied again. She had to take medication for a chemical imbalance in her brain. She often experienced a loss of past memories, particularly those of distant years.

"Why do I get the feeling that you're not being honest with me?" Jason questioned.

"I'm being honest. I have to run. I'll talk to you later." Victoria hung up the phone more confused than before. Someone must be behind this prank and she was sure of it. She nearly collapsed and placed her hands on her head in frustration. Moments later she regrouped and began looking into her past. She opened her laptop and did a google search for the family that had adopted her, the Blooms.

The search revealed millions of unwanted references. She decided to be more specific and google the Blooms Mining Company where her family made their fortune. But to Victoria's surprise, there was no match. She then searched Elana Bloom's name and found nothing. Victoria began to wonder if all this was real or make believe. She then decided to enter her name into the google search, wondering what she would do if her name could not be found; perhaps no name, family, adventures, or memories of any kind.

What if everything she'd known about her life was a lie? She hit enter and watched as the small loading wheel spun with anticipation. Every passing second seemed like an eternity, until it stopped. The gut-wrenching revelation hit her like an unstoppable train. There was no evidence that Victoria Bloom lived on this planet.

Victoria thought of the nonprofit foundation that her mother started in Yellow Knife, Canada. She googled the name Yellow Knife without any hits. When she searched for her hometown named Yellow Knife, she found a mental institution located in Chicago, Illinois. Victoria then retrieved the adoption papers from her dresser and was shocked by what she discovered. Yellow Knife wasn't a town in Canada, it was a psychiatric institution in Chicago. According to the adoption papers, Victoria was adopted from one of the institution's child transition centers. She then made arrangements to travel to Chicago for information regarding her adoption and the psychiatric institution.

CHAPTER THIRTY-FIVE

Smith

"What if I said you aren't real, but simply a void inside my head," Smith told Chanel.

"I would say that you've lost your mind," Chanel replied with a slight smile on her face.

Smith's face was stale and stoic with a ghost-like color and the energy of a dying soul. "I'm convinced that I'm going crazy and that you are part of my irrational thoughts." Smith held back her tears and rubbed her arm to create a distraction.

"I have no idea who told you these things, but I can assure you that I'm real." Chanel grabbed hold of Smith's hands and held them tightly. "Does this feel like I'm not real?" Chanel asked while Smith shook her head no.

"I'm real," Chanel assured her as she inched closer and kissed Smith's lips.

Smith closed her eyes, trying to embrace the moment and feel the passion that once flowed through her body. She even allowed Chanel to remove her shirt and undo her bra.

"Does this feel like I'm not here.?" Chanel asked as Smith let out a slight moan while Chanel's tongue licked around her nipples. Chanel got up and pulled Smith's pants and panties off.

"I love you," Chanel said while she kissed her thighs and felt the heat from Smith's vagina. Chanel removed all of her clothes and climbed Smith's body until their lips met and their eyes connected. Chanel then opened her mouth and allowed salvia to fall from her lips. Smith caught it and tasted the substance.

Chanel went back to kissing Smith while their tongues embraced. Smith welcomed Chanel's touch as her fingers slipped inside Smith's wet vagina. The juices filled Chanel's hand as she removed her fingers and tasted the nectar. Chanel climbed Smith's body until her snatch hovered above Smith's face. She lowered herself onto Smith's face and moaned while rocking in circular motions. Smith sucked and nibbled on Chanel's clitoris, imagining that she was eating into Chanel's soul. Chanel held onto Smith's head and grinded herself onto the face more aggressively as the pressure from an orgasm increased. Her moans grew in intensity and Smith pulled her ass cheeks apart to gain deeper penetration. Chanel came and covered Smith's mouth with her juices. The two of them devoured each other until they reached total exhaustion.

Smith watched Chanel as she slept, still convinced that Chanel was just a void created in her head. Smith got up from the bed and went to use the bathroom while she was still consumed by her thoughts. She figured if Chanel wasn't real then her drug habit was just a part of the void. She remembered finding a pouch filled with drug paraphernalia. Smith approached the cabinet and removed everything from it and pulled the glass shelves out. She pushed the hidden wall open and the pouch was gone. Smith was certain that no one knew of the secret compartment, but with that being the case, there was only one person who could have removed the pouch, and that was herself.

CHAPTER THIRTY-SIX

Chanel

I embraced my lover's touch and welcomed her with open arms; a feeling so intoxicating that I couldn't let go. Her love and compassion held on to my body. I've gone too long without her, not allowed to indulge her nor to roam freely through my body. I was in love all over again and this time I promised to never leave her again.

The heroin raced through her blood stream, causing her to rock back and forth as the euphoric plains opened the endless pastures of enchantment. Chanel discovered the all too familiar pouch in one of Smith's drawers, the pouch where she stored her drug paraphernalia. When she last overdosed and basically died, Smith found the pouch and removed it from her apartment. While Chanel had wrestled the temptation of using again, she finally broke down and entered the place of pleasures. She needed to escape from the torment she called life.

While Chanel had searched for a purpose throughout her life, she was unsuccessful and settled for the power of drugs to provide a temporary break from the daily torture. She had been running from everything that threatened her bell-being. While Chanel was mentally broken, there was nothing anyone could do about it.

Chanel was high and had no idea why she was calling Jasmine. "Hello?" Jasmine finally answered.

"I hear you're a big star now, all dolled up and twirling on that fancy stage," Chanel said. Jasmine knew from the sound of her voice that she was high. The slurring of her words, and the way she paused between each syllable was Jasmine's modus operandi.

"You caught me at a bad time. I got to go on the stage in less than five minutes."

"I can see you from right here," Chanel replied.

"Why?" Jasmine asked.

"Why what?"

"Why would you go back to using? You were doing so well," Jasmine said.

"Don't patronize me. Now that you're all self-righteous don't forget who took care of you when we were kids."

"We'll talk later, I have to go," Jasmine said.

"I love you." Chanel replied.

"I love you too," Jasmine replied and ended the call. Chanel managed to get to her feet and stagger towards the kitchen. She took the car keys from the counter and headed out the door. Once she made it to the car, she called the one person who occupied her thoughts. When she looked out the window, the sky opened as rain rushed from the sky. The silent rumbling and hidden illumination behind the clouds saddened her. Both the world and Chanel were hurting. She put her hand on the window and spoke in a whisper.

"I'm sorry you're sad."

"Meet me at the river," Chanel said and hung up.

*   *   *

OCTOBER 6, 2009

Casey shivered in the blanket as she tried to keep warm. As she followed her sister, Tianna, through the woods, her bones ached from the pain that cut through her small, fragile body. Tianna held Casey's hand and guided her towards the river.

"I got you. It's going to be okay. We're almost there." Tianna consoled her little sister. The morning fog was thick and heavy, allowing a scant level of visibility for anyone to see. But Tianna knew the woods like the back of her hand. Although she was only ten years old, she was mentally mature for her age.

Their mother, Jennifer, was a drunk and spent little time with her daughters. Tianna's young adventures often times led to hours and sometimes days when she was missing.

Years passed before Jennifer stopped drinking and began spending more time with the girls. But for Tianna, is was too late. She hated Jennifer and wanted nothing to do with her.

"Casey. Tianna." Jennifer called out. When she went to the girls' room, they were gone. She knew that Tianna spent most of her time in the woods, so she started to search for them.

"Momma's calling us," Casey said as she looked up at her sister.

"We'll meet her on the other side," Tianna replied.

"You promise?" Casey asked.

"Of course," Tianna replied. She knew her little sister was suffering from too much pain for any child to bear. Casey was all she had, and leukemia was a disease that played for keeps. The walk through the woods was rough and challenging for Casey's weak legs to hold up. The sounds of Jennifer's voice had become a distant cry. As Tianna carried her little sister on her back, they found a creek bed. They crossed it, and a short distance later, they came upon a rowboat. Tianna put Casey down and pushed the boat into the water.

"Come on," Tianna waved for Casey. But Casey was afraid of the water and expressed an unwillingness to enter the boat.

"It's okay," Tianna assured her. "I got you. Remember what I told you about love?" Tianna asked.

"It's all about trust, like having blind faith," Casey replied.

"Then trust me," Tianna said while extending her hand. When Casey grabbed hold of her sister's hand, the grip felt different, causing Casey to wonder if Tianna had become a complete stranger. At the moment, Casey did not fear the River. She was more afraid of the entity she perceived to be her very own flesh and blood. Tianna and Casey got into the boat and made for the open water.

"Where are we going?" Casey asked.

"To a place that'll make your pain go away," Tianna promised her.

"Okay," Casey replied, trying desperately to keep warm. They made it out to the middle of the river near the riverbank. She stopped the boat and looked at her sister.

"Why are we stopping?" Casey asked as she stared at her sister.

"Why are we stopping?" Casey asked a second time.

"You will never have to suffer again. I promise," Tianna said while reaching out to Casey's small, fragile body. As she held Casey, she felt her shivering in her arms. Tianna hated what had to be done, but it was for the best. She knew Casey would die from her condition and she didn't want to see her suffer any longer.

"What are you doing?" Casey asked as Tianna picked her up. Tianna didn't reply. Casey then tried to resist being lowered into the river. She clawed and scratched at Tianna's arm. The piercing cries carried across the river's surface like those of a wounded coyote. In the midst of Tianna's struggle to push Casey into the water, she heard her mother yelling from the riverbank. While Casey struggled even more, tears ran down Tianna's face.

As Tianna pulled Casey's tiny hands from the boat, Casey struggled to stay afloat as her lungs filled with water, pulling her deeper into the abyss. The splash near the riverbank was loud and sudden. Jennifer had jumped into the river and tried to swim towards Casey, but the harder she tried, the more her body descended below the water's surface. Although Jennifer couldn't swim, it was a mother's will that encouraged her to try and reach Casey before it was too late. Tianna watched as Casey's body began to fade. It was painful to watch her sister drown, but it was the only way she could save Casey from all of the pain. The look in Casey's eyes told her that she had forgiven her. Although it pained her a great deal, Tianna understood what needed to be done. Jennifer was only collateral damage. She died in the same river as Casey. The swells washed away their existence and the short burst of waves settled amongst the under currents that claimed their lives. It was a sad day, one that would haunt Tianna forever.

CHAPTER THIRTY-SEVEN

Tianna

DAM.NANT QUOD NON INTELLIGUNT is a Latin saying: "They condemn what they do not understand." My past — easily misjudged — was a revulsion that never stopped haunting me. I drowned in my distractions; created a make-believe path and never deviated from the course I chose. An imaginary cocoon sought to protect my broken and tormented soul. But my actions weren't callous nor malicious. They were created for one purpose only — make my little sister's pain disappear. Why else would I drown my sister and claim that I loved her all in the same breath?

No one saw what I witnessed when I looked into Casey's eyes and grasped the pain in her fragile body. While I wanted it to stop, there was no other way. Casey had been sentenced to a life-long struggle with a predictable ending; she was destined to die.

OCTOBER 6, 2009 CONTINUED...

Casey's eyes were frozen open, impossible to shut, as if her soul watched the betrayal of her assailant. Fighting the inevitable was pointless. Casey saw the fire burning in Tianna's eyes; the clarity of her decision; and that Casey understood why Tianna was committed to killing her. After a brief struggle to live, Casey forgave Tianna and slowly slipped into a darkened place; a bright-shinning, light glowed in the distance.

Echoes of Jennifer's mournful cries bellowed throughout the woods and glanced off the cold surface of *"The Black River."* Jennifer jumped off the riverbank and into the river with the determination of a mother destined to save her child. But in Jennifer's haste, she didn't consider the fact that she didn't know how to swim. The further she moved from the shore, the stronger the undercurrents sucked her body downward. The sounds of her efforts to expel the water from her lungs became Tianna's reoccurring memory.

A father and son were hunting in the woods and heard the screams. They quickly determined that a woman called out to her children in a rowboat north of the riverbank. The duo witnessed one of the girls throw the smaller one into the river. While the smaller girl fought with her limited strength, she quickly fell victim to the inevitable.

The father told his son to call the police and tell them to bring an ambulance. He passed the rifle to his son and ran down the steep hill towards the river. He then dove into the river and swam straight to the rowboat. He found the girl's body and carried her to the riverbank where his son was waiting.

"Pull her out," the father ordered. "Now son, pull her out," his father yelled. The young boy grabbed hold of the lifeless body. Casey was so small and fragile that the father was afraid to touch her in fear of breaking her ribs. But he had no choice. He administered CPR and pushed against her tiny chest as ribs could be heard cracking with each compression.

"Come on. Breathe angel." Just when he thought there was no hope, Casey began coughing and spitting up water. The father sat her up and told her everything would be alright. He then picked her up and ran up the steep hill and down the road until he saw some flashing lights. Casey was taken to the hospital while the police picked up Tianna at the scene. The father and son explained what they had witnessed, and a dive team was called out. While they found Jennifer's lifeless body, there was nothing more they could do for her.

Although Tianna was very upset when the detectives began to question her, she freely shared a belief that she was helping Casey and that killing her was the right thing to do. She advised them of Casey's condition and that drowning was the only way to end her pain. When the detectives told Tianna that Casey wasn't dead and was in the hospital, Tianna entered a fit of rage. It was apparent that Tianna was a troubled and unstable woman. They ended the interview.

This was a dark day for the residents of a small township located in the hills of northern California. They shared stories to the local, state, and national media. The headline was clear: *"Big sister kills little sister, and mother drowns."* The crime scene became known as, *"The Black River."*

* * *

Small drops of water fell from the faucet, hitting the puddle that refused to go down the drain. The old house was aging and subjected to poor management. It was an earlier time when Tianna and Casey were little girls doing what kids do. They liked hiding underneath their make-shift tent constructed of sheets, pillows, and blankets, watching mice crawl under the door and eat the breadcrumbs that they had tossed onto the floor.

Jennifer was an absentee mother, never home long enough to make a sandwich or prepare a balanced meal for the girls. Tianna picked up the slack and did her best to keep Casey comfortable. She loved her sister and vowed to protect her.

"If you could be anybody in the world, who would you be?" Tianna asked.

"I'd just be a normal kid. How about you?" Casey answered.

"I'd be a rich girl from Canada. My name would be Victoria Bloom and I'd live in a huge mansion," Tianna explained while putting emphasis on a huge mansion by spreading her arms out. "I would have a butler, maids, and a mother I'd be close to."

"And what would her name be?" Casey inquired.

Tianna thought for a minute before answering. "Elana Bloom, but I'd call her Lana for short."

"Sounds nice," Casey added as she closed her eyes. "Can I be a dolphin instead of a person?" Casey asked.

"Why a dolphin," Tianna asked.

"I don't know. Maybe because I like them and they're great swimmers," Casey said. "Do you think I'm going to die," Casey suddenly and without warning asked.

"No, you're going to be fine," Tianna replied unconvincingly.

"You can tell me the truth, it's okay. Just promise me this. If I suffer, just make it stop."

"I promise," Tianna said while wiping away her tears. While Tianna was strong, it was painful to watch her sister battle a disease she didn't asked for. Life wasn't fair, and if Tianna could take her sister's place, she would not hesitate.

"You'll be alright kiddo," Tianna said and kissed her forehead. Tianna noticed a slight smile on her face while she fought the pain and showed her gratitude at the same time.

> There's a language hidden in colors, spoken in a variety of shades. But we're not hardwired to think beyond the realms of simplicity, let alone find an understanding amongst life's intricate details. The vast majority of people have an appetite for the simple, and there's nothing wrong with being modest. Just don't shit on the aspirations of the dreamers who think outside the box and beyond the sky.
>
> Dying is the easy part; not having to endure the hardships and painful losses that were your calling. I'm just another cog in life's cycle, waiting to be chewed-up and expelled by its unforgiving nature. Needless to say, I don't give a fuck about dying and neither should you.

CHAPTER THIRTY-EIGHT

Chanel And Victoria

Victoria's position in the world was confusing and uncertain; who and what was she? It was time for clarity. Tracing her path from the adoption agency to her current status seemed logical. But for now, she was on her way to meet Chanel at the river.

Hours later, Victoria found herself at the top of a hill. She parked her car and followed the instructions that Chanel had given her. She walked down the hill and approached the riverbank where Chanel stood waiting.

Chanel was still high and feeling the effects of the heroin running through her body. She felt elevated to a level higher than the clouds; a special place where the spirited-ones fly. They made contact and exchanged smiles. Chanel knew that Victoria was in love with her from the first time they had met.

"This river has an interesting story, one that I would never forget," Chanel said.

"I'm sure it's quite the story," Victoria replied.

"Right around that ridge to the north of us, a little girl was drowned by her big sister, and their mother drowned as well. The world painted her out to be a monster for killing her little sister. The mother jumped in the river from this exact spot, trying to reach the little girl. She tried to make it to the little girl but had forgotten that she didn't know how

196

to swim. The little girl and the mother both drowned, and the older sister was locked away in a mental institution. They say she was fucked up in the head," Chanel said with a slight chuckle.

"That's a sad story," Victoria replied.

"The locals referred to the crime scene as *"The Black River,"* Chanel explained. "They believed the river to be a source of bad energy and warned people not to swim in this unforgiving place."

* * *

Victoria watched the rough-water hug the riverbank. The sun retired for the day and the river gave birth to short bursts of waves that threatened the shore. Mother Nature's elements of tranquility and destruction were on full display. Victoria's eyes pierced the water's surface as she studied the river snaking through pastures and open plains. Barricades dared not to confine its flow.

When Victoria was young, large bodies of water threatened her well-being. So much so that she barred herself from diving into the mysteries that lie below the river's surface. Time revealed the reason for her fears. Someone or something lived in the darkened waters that threatened her safety. But don't blame Victoria for having a dysfunctional childhood and an overly creative mind. Her brain was hardwired to think irrationally.

Something was off that day; a gut-wrenching and unnerving kind of off. Victoria blamed herself for what happened when she met Chanel at the river. While all of the signs were there, it was a time of confusion when 2 equals 1.

"Are you scared?" Chanel asked. "You're shaking."

Victoria knew that she was afraid. As the two of them stood on the water's edge watching the currents race by, there was an eerie silence. Victoria didn't know why, but she had told Chanel that she wasn't afraid.

Chanel had an energy that was quite alluring; an adrenaline junkie who danced along the edges of danger. Each adventure was accompanied by a spiritual energy as if she was suddenly reborn. Her breathing became more labored and her heart was on fire. Victoria grabbed Chanel's hands that were cold and unwelcoming as if she had touched a stranger. They faced each other; so close that their heartbeats were in unison. As their lips touched, Victoria remembered the passion that burned deep into her soul; spellbound and persuaded by the words that Chanel never spoke; eyes that shared a telling tale; and private things that remained hidden from the world.

Chanel's demeanor morphed into an emptiness disconnected from reality. Is this the person who Victoria had known to be Chanel, or was she an illusion?

"Do you love me?" Chanel questioned. She gripped Victoria's hand tighter as if she dared her to tell a lie.

"Of course, I love you," Victoria answered. But the grip of Chanel's hand was different, causing Victoria to wonder if Chanel had become a complete stranger. At the moment, Victoria did not fear the river. She was more afraid of the entity she perceived to be Chanel.

"Why would you ask if I loved you?" Victoria asked.

"Because I need to know."

"Yes, I love you. But you know that already. You're acting strange and freaking me out," Victoria admitted.

Chanel's laugh was accompanied by a sinister smile. "If you love me, jump, jump into the river," Chanel commanded. "Love is all about trust, right?"

"I will drown," Victoria replied. "I can't swim, you know that."

"Trust me," Chanel explained." I would never allow anything bad to happen to you."

Victoria felt overcome by emotions knowing that she needed to escape before it was too late. While she remembered fragments of what happened that day, she preferred to believe that Chanel pushed her into the river. Given Victoria's fear of the river, that made more sense. But reality told a different story. Victoria jumped into the river.

Stupidity is oftentimes driven by ignorance, a compelling force that causes us to defy logic. Perhaps a need to display her courage was why Victoria jumped into the river, or was it love interlinked with confusion?

A blind fondness accompanied by faith creates the foundation for love. But reckless love ignores your core, leaving you to think only of the image you desire; the one that caused Victoria to jump into the river.

Chanel stood on the shore watching Victoria struggle to evade the adversity she had feared since her childhood — drowning in the river. Her attempts to scream were muffled by the sheer volume of water. Most people who fear the possibility of death by drowning, stay away from large bodies of water. But not Victoria, she jumped into the river.

Victoria's mind held no clarity or reasoning for what was happening to her. She felt the burning sensation a body experiences when your lungs take on water. The image of the river changed as she began to accept her fate. The deeper parts of the river were calm and without motion, unlike the chaotic movements of the river's surface. The struggle to survive diminished as her body sank towards the river's floor.

Victoria remembered seeing Chanel through the water's surface; lips parted with a smile on her face. At that moment Victoria's heart no longer beat; not from drowning but from a broken heart. Chanel killed Victoria before the water filled her lungs and severed her oxygen supply.

She then experienced a more peaceful world as her body embraced the river's floor. She looked up through the surface and saw Chanel standing at the water's edge. No longer angered. Victoria was at peace. Now as Victoria accepted her fate, she saw the two of them standing side by side; both one in the same, when 2 equals 1.

*   *   *

The truth is, I didn't die that day and I never existed. As for Victoria, there was no luxurious mansion, private jets, large bank accounts. It all filled a void created in her head. We're all the same, just different stories in the same vacuity and serfage. All of our stories end in carnage; undone by reality taking hold of the altered realms where such voids existed. So maybe I did die, the part of me which belonged to a specific set of memories. Now it's all just washed away with the tides being flushed down the cycle.

But I finally saw the two of them together, standing at the edge of that riverbank as the water pulled me under. I saw them, I saw Chanel and Casey watching me drown, watching my void being filled with water. Maybe now Casey's soul could be at rest and Chanel could move on with her life or was she just another void as well?

CHAPTER THIRTY-NINE

Tianna

I danced along the shadows of death
as if nothing was left.
As if I'd taken my last breath.
Slowly waiting for my name to be called
by that awful sound of death.
Holding my breath,
As I danced along the shadow of death.
Smiling a crooked smile of carnage,
mayhem gaining ground like nothing is left.
I danced, and I danced.

Tianna sat with her foot on the accelerator and the car in neutral. All of the windows were lowered, and the garage filled with smoke. Her world had been turned upside down. Thoughts of what happened that day in *"The Black River"* played over and over through her mind; a massive migraine and an aggressive heartbeat occupied her head. How could she have done such a thing?

Tianna's tear-filled eyes made it difficult for her to see what she had written. She needed the world to know that she wasn't a monster. She did, in fact, suffer from a severe mental illness.

The smoke began to fill the car. Tianna coughed and fought back the urge to bolt from the garage. The tears kept running while the memories raced through her head. The image of Casey's eyes as she left the water's surface was edged into her memories to be replayed over and over. Tianna then grabbed the steering wheel with both hands and accepted her fate. Casey was gone and it was all her fault.

Tianna closed her eyes from the burning fumes and allowed the carbon dioxide to invade her lungs. She felt light-headed, imagining the gift to float into the open skies and unleash her wings; gliding through the pasture's plush clouds and soothing winds. She then recalled hearing Casey's laugh; the light, airy sound of a faint, belly laugh. They were playing around their house, just being kids.

Tianna fell back against the car seat as her arms went limp and her pen fell onto the car floor.

*   *   *

TO WHOEVER FINDS THIS:

If you're reading this then that means I'm already dead. I took my own life for the unspeakable chain of events that claimed both the lives of my sister and mother. Realizing that I was sick and what I'd done came years later, and it drove me insane. The truth is, I wanted it all to stop, for it to go away and allow Casey to be a normal kid. I promised her that she wouldn't suffer. She never asked to be brought into this world let alone be born with a disease that riddled her body with agonizing pain. I just wanted to help, to make it all stop. I didn't intend on my mother to come looking for us that day. Her death was senseless, and now we're all subjected to the same fate.

I don't want to be remembered as a monster, because that's the furthest thing from the truth. When my story is told to the world, let it be known that I cared. That I tried to make the pain end and I never meant for things to happen the way they did.

CHAPTER FORTY

Jasmine

Jasmine sat on the edge of the bathtub and wiped her runny nose. She had been under the weather with a slight fever. Jasmine was focused on the play's first performance, trying to maintain her motivation and hide her illness. It had to be a cold or possibly a mild case of the flu, Jasmine thought.

She hadn't heard nor seen Chanel in quite some time. Jasmine and Amber had been shacking up. Since the two of them shared roles in the play, it was convenient to stay together and rehearse. While the stage director was a man without a conscience, he ran a tight ship; better known for his creative vision and ability to bring out the best from each performer.

As the dancers twirled in and out of the scene, the dancers switched accordingly.

"Ballet company — swans." He yelled and the stage suddenly shifted with a fresh set of legs.

"Protagonist, where's my protagonist?" He raged on.

"Amber, you're up," he added. She gracefully took to the stage and embraced her role effortlessly. Her movements were captivating and alluring.

"Jasmine, you're on," the director shouted. Her entrance was swift; gradually syncing with Amber as the two of them met up in the center of the stage.

"More energy Jasmine. Move your boney ass!" he yelled. Amber gave Jasmine a look of concern. Normally the two of them would be tied to the same wave of energy as if they were one body. Jasmine made an early turn and as she did, she came down on one of her toes. While she cringed in agony, she continued dancing as if nothing was wrong. She knew it was broken, but after all, she was a dancer. Amber knew something was up and that Jasmine was holding back.

"Move it, move it, move it. I want to see more movement," screamed the director.

As Jasmine danced across the stage, she felt herself growing lighter by the second. The noise around her faded. It was just her on the stage dancing as if there wasn't a care in the world. She felt the energy and vibrations from the music as it flowed through her body. The one place where she felt comfortable and at peace was about to end. The music faded into silence; the lights dimmed darkness; and Jasmine moved toward the exit and passed out.

*　*　*

Hours passed before Jasmine opened her eyes. She was in the hospital with no memory of what had happened while she was on stage. As she tried to make sense of what had transpired, Amber walked into the room.

"You scared me back there." That was the only thing she could say.

"What happened?" Jasmine asked.

"Don't know. You just passed out."

"I'm sure that was the talk of the town," Jasmine replied.

"What's going on with you?" Amber questioned.

"I'm just stressed," Jasmine lied. Amber noticed her questionable answer and decided to leave it alone. She took a seat next to the bed and with a forced smile on her face.

"Thanks for being here," Jasmine added.

"Of course."

"I was a bit out of it today on that stage. I think my toe is broken." Jasmine tried to add a bit of humor to her comment. Amber laughed and commented on how swollen it was.

"The first show is next week. You're not going to be ready," Amber said.

"I will. Trust me on that," Jasmine snapped back.

"I'm not the one that you have to convince. The director feels your energy has dropped off over the past two of weeks."

"I guess I'm not entitled to have a stretch of bad days," Jasmine commented.

"As a professional dancer, no! It's like you've lost your fire. I don't see that grit or passion anymore," Amber added.

"Well I'm sorry that I can't please you either," Jasmine snapped back.

"That's not fair Jasmine. I'm not trying to be hard on you. I just feel that you should know the truth," Amber replied. The doctor walked in and asked how Jasmine was feeling. His face reflected a feeling of sadness.

"Do you mind if I speak with her in private?" the doctor asked Amber.

"It's fine, you can speak freely with her," Jasmine assured him. The doctor cleared his throat and spoke clearly.

"I ran some tests on your blood work which is standard procedure for patients who've been admitted due to blackouts. In doing so, we discovered antibodies and decided to test you for H.I.V. The results came back positive."

"That can't be right. You have to run that again." Jasmine was in shock. Amber's stomach turned and her knees nearly buckled.

"We ran the test multiple times and they all came back positive. Ms. Winters, you're entering the next phase of the disease. You're on the verge of full-blown aids. At this point, the only option is to make you comfortable," the doctor explained.

"How long do I have?" Jasmine asked with a quiet, shaking voice.

"Six months at the most," the doctor replied.

Amber ran out of the room in disbelief. Jasmine was given a death sentence and there was nothing she could do about it.

"I'm sorry," the doctor said as he walked out of the room. Jasmine was numb and disconnected from her emotions. While she'd been given a one-way trip to the white light, Chanel was the one most responsible.

There was a knock on Jasmine's door. A man dressed in a suit entered and introduced himself as detective Kevin Johnson.

"Jasmine Winters, right?" he casually asked. He had no idea what was running through her head, that she'd just been advised that she had six months to live.

"Yes, what is this about?"

"Do you know this woman?" The detective showed Jasmine a photograph of Chanel.

"Yes, that's my friend."

"When was the last time you heard from her?" he asked.

"About a week ago, why?" Concern came over Jasmine's face.

"We noticed her last outgoing calls were all to your number. We found her dead in her garage. She committed suicide. Carbon dioxide," the detective explained.

At that moment, Jasmine felt a crack open-up in her heart.

> I didn't see our lives ending like this. Chanel and I were so vibrant, driven towards all the elements it took to be successful. The writings on the wall were there all along. Tianna was sick. While she lived inside her head, I tried to be there for her and understand what she saw, and how she thought. Victoria Bloom, and Chanel Rosenthal were all the same imaginary people. There were no endless supply of money, no billion dollar companies, and no childhood in Canada. It was all made up. Chanel was just another imaginary personality to fill the void in Tianna Smith's head.
>
> I had no idea who she was, and I really didn't care. I just know that the two of us understood each other, and our love for one another was genuine. I could have saved her, but I ignored the signs and chose to indulge in her fucked up world. While

Chanel was beautiful inside and out, she was lost. The two of us were broken and discarded. We were both lost.

* * *

While Jasmine cried, the good times flashed through her head. They shared a connection that only comes once in an eon. Jasmine now believed that dying wasn't such a bad thing. The two of them would find each other again and take the afterlife by storm.

EPILOGUE

Jasmine

SIX MONTHS LATER...

We're all broken in one way or the other; tied to something both dreadful and pleasing. Perhaps the winds carry us like the feathers from an eagle's wing, or the stale smell of devastation harnesses our mind in an unrelenting manner. Our path is determined by choices we make, tainted by fate, and influenced by mind-altering drugs. The yin and yang, the balance between good and evil, is a lifelong struggle full of winners and losers. My postmortem examination will judge me as well; a young woman infected by Human Immunodeficiency Virus (HIV), poisoned by fate, grim decisions, and a bucketful of street drugs, is about to die. But when all is said and done, I had some fucking good times.

I don't fault Tianna, Chanel, or Victoria for my predetermined death sentence. But I must say that Tianna's severe mental illness most definitely shaped our lives. Tianna was the puppeteer who gave birth to Victoria and Chanel and defined who we became. She filled the void — the empty spot in her brain — with real and imaginary characters. Each of us, whether real or not, were portrayed as sane individuals with the typical social interactions that humans face. Tianna was the broken one; overwhelmed by the memory of killing her little sister.

Although Tianna was the source of our existence, Chanel was the glue that held us together. Her street smarts, together with her ability to compartmentalize her trauma, allowed her to survive in a dysfunctional world. Chanel and I first met in the Yellow Knife Psychiatric Ward, a mental institution for juveniles; often times called a prison for children. It was obvious that Chanel held a mature presence well-beyond her chronological age. My strength, determination, and survival skills were gifts from Chanel. Despite her strengths, she suffered from a mental illness that took her down. Instead of medication, she chose her high energy, wildness, and a love for heroin to serve as her coping mechanisms against insanity. While I knew she was fucked-up and would most likely harm my mental health, I loved her like no other.

Victoria was the polar opposite of Chanel. She was more reserved and succinct; a role-model for someone into numbers and business ventures. Victoria, the girl from Canada, was captivated by a search for her identify as an adopted child. I know we could have been friends if we had more time.

*   *   *

"I need to tell my story," Jasmine said as she lie in a hospital bed. She had been diagnosed with HIV and given a maximum of six months to live. Her beautiful body had been reduced to a mere fifty-pound shell. Still, her mind was alive and yearning to share her story. She spent the past six months sharing her experience with Layuh, a recent college graduate and a freelance journalist. Little did Jasmine know that this would be her final interview before she died. In spite of her physical condition, she spoke in soft but powerful words.

A nurse gave Jasmine a sip of water as she struggled to clear her throat. She then placed an additional pillow under Jasmine's head and covered her with a warm blanket. The steady beeping sound of the heart rate monitor provided a reminder that Jasmine was still alive.

"Whatever happened to Amber?" Layuh asked. "Did she contract HIV as well?" Jasmine didn't answer right away. Instead, she closed her eyes and thought about the good times that she and Amber spent together. Tears trickled down her face as she embraced her sadness.

"I have no idea," Jasmine replied. "After she stormed out of my hospital room, I never heard from her again. I didn't bother to call. Besides, what was there to say? I understood her anger and rage. I felt the same way about Chanel," Jasmine explained.

"I'm sorry," Layuh said.

"You don't have to be," Jasmine replied.

"Did you attend Chanel's funeral?" Layuh asked.

"Dying isn't easy, especially for those who lived on the edge like the two of us," Jasmine explained. "While Chanel was broken, I knew she wouldn't give up. The thought of dying scared her more than anything. We both came from a toxic environment and understood what it felt like to be denied and abandoned. The world was relentless and cold. That was our bond."

"Chanel was a complicated and confident woman. I couldn't envision her in a box being lowered into the ground and covered with dirt. I had to let her go on her own terms and to let things unravel the way they did. But I'm sure I will see her soon," Jasmine said with a slight smile on her washed-out face.

"So, what will you call this story?" Jasmine wanted to know.

"*The Black River*, I'll call it *The Black River*," Layuh said as the rain and thunder suddenly appeared. Jasmine removed the covers from her body and used what strength was left to get out of bed and walk to the window. Her fragile legs moved slowly as Layuh helped her with each step.

Jasmine raised her hand and placed it on the window and spoke, "I'm sorry you're sad." She began to cough and wheeze as her condition moved from stable to terminal.

"Let's get you back to bed," Layuh suggested. This would be the last time Jasmine witnessed a thunderstorm, smelled the wet grass, and played in the rain.

"I want you to promise me that you'll tell Amber my story. Ask her to forgive me," Jasmine said. Two nurses and a doctor rushed to Jasmine's room.

The thunder roared and growled, and the lightening lit the sky. The heavens played its final symphony as Jasmine closed her eyes.

"The Shadow of Death"

Maybe one day we'll meet again
and unravel in the world of bliss.
The lingering bitterness holds me together
like your touch and welcoming kiss.
The breeze from entangled trees
remind me of our bond.
Charmed by your passion and fondness,
maybe one day we can meet again,
find each other and unwind.
Love ourselves and rediscover
who we are.
We can walk alone the shadow of death,
and dance until there's nothing left.